Reading for Interest

FUN AND FROLIC

D. C. HEATH AND COMPANY

Boston

The stories and poems in this book were selected by

BARBARA NOLEN

and illustrated by

EMMA BROCK

Educational Consultants

PAUL WITTY and FLORENCE BRUMBAUGH

Reading for Interest

PAUL WITTY, *of Northwestern University, has served as consultant for this series, co-operating with the educators whose names appear beneath the titles listed below.*

Ned and Nancy, by Inez Hogan. Illustrated by Corinne Malvern.
 KATE KELLY, State Normal School, Castleton, Vermont

Bigger and Bigger, by Inez Hogan. Illustrated by the author.
 KATE KELLY, State Normal School, Castleton, Vermont

Little Lost Dog, by Lula Wright. Illustrated by Winifred Bromhall.
 KATE KELLY, State Normal School, Castleton, Vermont

Play at Home, by Louise E. Broaddus. Illustrated by Mario Rendina.
 LOUISE E. BROADDUS, Public Schools, Richmond, Virginia

A Home for Sandy, by Romney Gay. Illustrated by the author.
 LULA WRIGHT, Lincoln School, New York City

Rain and Shine, by Ardra Soule Wavle. Illustrated by Ruth Steed.
 ETHEL MABIE FALK, Author and Lecturer, Madison, Wisconsin

Something Different, by Eva Knox Evans. Illustrated by Pelagie Doane.
 ETTA ROSE BAILEY, Matthew Maury School, Richmond, Virginia

Lost and Found, by Robin Palmer. Illustrated by Edna Potter.
 RUTH BRISTOL, State Teachers College, Milwaukee, Wisconsin

Fun and Frolic, Barbara Nolen, Editor. Illustrated by Emma Brock.
 FLORENCE BRUMBAUGH, Hunter College Elementary School, New York City

Luck and Pluck, Barbara Nolen, Editor. Illustrated by Decie Merwin.
 DOROTHY K. CADWALLADER, Carroll Robbins School, Trenton, New Jersey

Merry Hearts and Bold, Barbara Nolen, Editor. Illustrated by Fritz Kredel.
 PHYLLIS FENNER, Public Schools, Manhasset, New York

The Brave and Free, Barbara Nolen, Editor. Illustrated by Harve Stein.
 URSULA BRINGHURST, New York University, New York City

CONTENTS

Up and Down the Road

vi

UP AND DOWN THE ROAD

TINKER'S ADVENTURES

There was once a tiger cat with yellow eyes and white paws. His name was Tinker and he lived at a farm near a lake.

Nobody asked Tinker if he wanted to go to the city when fall came. He wanted to stay on the farm with Aunt Aggie and Uncle Bill, but the children took him to the city just the same.

Tinker didn't like the train.

He didn't like the new house in the city.

"I want to go back to Aunt Aggie," he said, as soon as he had looked around.

3

The first time the door was open, Tinker started off. He wore his walking shoes and carried all his things in a red handkerchief. He had a present for Aunt Aggie, too.

Being very careful, he crept through the city, but then he came to a great big river. Alas! It was too wide for any cat to swim.

There was a bridge over the great big river, and a toll-gate house at the nearer end. The toll-gate man looked out of his little window when he saw Tinker.

"What's a cat doing here, all alone?" he asked.

"I want to go home to the farm," mewed Tinker.

"You want to go home!" said the man. "Who will pay your toll?"

"I don't know," mewed Tinker sadly. "I have no money."

"Well," said the man, "never mind about the toll. After all, cats don't have to pay toll."

And the toll-gate man let Tinker go by.

The bridge was high, the river was wide, and Tinker felt very small. But he got across.

On the other side, the open country began. Tinker picked up a little stick so that he could carry his handkerchief over his shoulder. This made walking easier. But the road was long and the sun was hot. Tinker stopped often to rest.

In the middle of the morning, he met a frog at a little pond where he stopped to drink.

"How far is it to Sunset Lake?" he asked. He was sure that a frog would know all about water.

"Two million jumps," answered the frog.

Tinker didn't know how far that would be, but he walked on.

At one farm a great dog sprang out, barking.

Tinker ran for his life, but he remembered to run north.

At supper time, Tinker sat down on a stone, took a catnip sandwich from his bundle, and ate it. It was all he had been able to bring.

Then he licked his whiskers clean, and started down the road again.

It grew very dark, with woods on each side of the road, but Tinker's eyes shone through the dark like two little yellow lights.

Suddenly an owl hooted from a tree.

"Who are you? Who are you? Who are you?" hooted the owl.

"I'm Tinker, going home," purred the cat.

"Too big to eat! Too big to eat!" the owl hooted again.

Tinker's little feet went pitter patter, pitter patter, all night long. On, on, on he went, all through the night.

In the early morning a truck driver asked him if he wanted a ride.

"No, thank you," said Tinker politely. He knew he was a very fine cat, and he didn't want to be carried off by a stranger.

As the sun grew hotter and hotter, Tinker walked more slowly. The sun was burning his whiskers. Anyone could see that he was tired.

A kind white cat, sitting in a garden, called out to him and asked, "Are you hungry?"

Tinker had a dish of milk with the kind white cat. He was asked to stay, but he mewed sadly, "I must go home."

In the afternoon a great rain came pouring down. Tinker was so wet that the color came out of his red handkerchief and ran down his paws.

His shoes hurt so much that at last he took

them off and hid them in a stone wall. He might come that way again and want them. Now he knew that he could not be very far from home.

Hurry, hurry, went Tinker's tired little feet. Hurry, hurry, went his little heart. He came to a field where he used to prowl. And there on the hill was his own farm with the lake beyond.

Tinker ran faster than he had ever run before. Then suddenly he stopped. He sat down and washed and dusted his coat and tail. He tied his handkerchief in a new knot.

When Aunt Aggie came out to feed the chickens, he walked up to her as though he had never been away at all.

"Tinker!" cried Aunt Aggie. "What are you doing here? I thought you were miles and miles away in the city."

"Oh, I just thought I'd come home," purred Tinker. He looked up at Aunt Aggie and held out the ring he had brought her from the city.

Elizabeth Coatsworth

THE FALLING STAR

I saw a star slide down the sky,
Blinding the north as it went by,
Too burning and too quick to hold,
Too lovely to be bought or sold,
Good only to make wishes on
And then forever to be gone.

Sara Teasdale

THE LITTLE SCARECROW BOY

Once upon a time, in a cornfield, there lived a scarecrow and his scarecrow wife and their little scarecrow boy.

Every day of the world, Old Man Scarecrow would go out into the cornfield to make faces at the crows. And every day of the world, Little Scarecrow Boy would want to come, too. And every day of the world, Old Man Scarecrow would say:

"No!
No, little boy,
You can't go.
You're not fierce enough
To scare a crow.
Wait until you grow."

So—Little Scarecrow Boy would have to stay at home all day and just grow.

Every day, out in the cornfield, Old Man Scarecrow waved his arms and made terrible faces. He made such terrible faces that the crows would fly far, far away at the sight of him there.

Every evening, when the sun went down, Old Man Scarecrow would come home. All evening he would sit in his scarecrow house, teaching Little Scarecrow Boy how to make fierce faces. Old Lady Scarecrow would whistle through her straw teeth at the looks of them there.

But early in the morning, when the sun came up, it was the same old story:

"No!

No, little boy,

You can't go.

You're not fierce enough

To scare a crow.

Wait until you grow."

So—Little Scarecrow Boy had to stay at home all day and just grow.

Then, one day, after the little boy knew all six of his father's terrible faces so that he could make them one after the other, he decided to run away. He decided to go out into the cornfield and frighten a crow.

So—the next morning, before the sun was up, or Old Man Scarecrow was up, or Old Lady Scarecrow was up, Little Scarecrow Boy slipped out of bed. He dressed and went quietly, quietly, quietly, out of the house and over to the cornfield. He climbed up on the post in his father's place.

It was a fine morning, with the sun shining on the tall green corn. Far away over the trees, crows flew around and around. Little Scarecrow Boy waved his arms through the air. He had never felt fiercer in all his life.

And then came flying a big black crow.

"Oh! Oh! Oh!" said Little Scarecrow Boy, and he made his first fierce face.

Still came flying the big black crow.

"Oh! Oh! Oh!" Little Scarecrow Boy made his second fierce face.

Still came flying the big black crow.

He made his third fierce face. "Oh! Oh! Oh!"

It was time to go.

So—Little Scarecrow Boy ran and ran down the cornfield. Looking back, he could see the big black crow up in the sky.

He ran and he ran. Then he stopped.

He made his fourth fierce face.

Still came flying the big black crow.

So—he ran and he ran and he ran and he ran.

And the crow flew and he flew and he flew and he flew.

As Little Scarecrow Boy ran, he made his fifth fierce face. The next one would be the last, and it would be the fiercest face of all.

Still came flying the big black crow.

Little Scarecrow Boy had only one face left now and hardly any breath. Even so, he stopped. He stretched his arms wide above his head. He made his sixth face!

Whoa! The old crow flew backwards through the air, feathers flying everywhere, until there wasn't even the shadow of a crow in the cornfield.

A scarecrow at last! Little Scarecrow Boy knew that he was now a fierce scarecrow, as fierce as his father. He was as fierce a scarecrow as there was in all the cornfields in all the world.

Then Little Scarecrow Boy saw a shadow in front of him and he looked around. There behind him, as he made the sixth fierce face, was his

father. Old Man Scarecrow was proud of his little boy, who had made all six faces at the crow. He picked him up in his scarecrow arms and carried him home to breakfast. And when Little Scarecrow Boy grew up, he was the fiercest scarecrow in all the cornfields in all the world.

Margaret Wise Brown

17

THE BLACK CAT AND THE PUMPKIN

The terrific terrible pumpkin,
With the zigzag, zigzag grin,
Met a cat
And that was that.
Now watch the fight begin.

"I'll scratch out your eyes,"
Said the scratching cat.
"I'll scratch out your eyes
And tear up your chin."

Then the terrific terrible pumpkin
Smiled his zigzag grin.
"I haven't any eyes," he said,
"And I haven't any chin."

Margaret Wise Brown

OLD SNAPPER

Look Out for Danger

One summer morning, some little snapping turtles were swimming among the cattails at the edge of a large swamp. These little turtles were only a few days old, and the swamp was a strange and wonderful place to them.

"See how straight and still the cattails stand," said one, stretching his head far out of his shell. "They don't move about as we do."

"Hear the frogs," said another. "What loud voices they have!"

"It's fun to live in the swamp, isn't it?" said a third. "There are so many things to see."

19

"Sh!" said a fourth. "Here comes Old Snapper. Let's be quiet."

The little turtles swam quickly in among the cattails and looked out at an old turtle crawling slowly along a big mossy log not far away. They had seen Old Snapper many times in the past few days, but they had always taken care to keep out of his way. He was so big that he frightened them. Now they watched him as he crawled out to the end of the log and closed his eyes for a nap.

"He looks cross," one of the little turtles said at last. "Let's swim over to the other side of the pond."

The littlest turtle of all spoke up quickly. "I don't think he looks cross," he said. "I'm going over and talk to him."

"Don't do it," the others told him. "He might not like it."

"I'm not afraid," said the littlest turtle and swam quickly away.

He reached the log on which Old Snapper was

taking a nap. Then he climbed and crawled up beside the old turtle.

"Good morning," he said. "How are you this morning, Old Snapper?"

"Can't you see I am trying to take a nap?" Old Snapper asked without opening his eyes.

He sounded so cross that for a moment the littlest turtle wanted to go back to the cattails. But it would never do to run away while the other little turtles were watching, so he said politely, "I'm sorry if I woke you, but now that you are awake, do you mind if I ask you something?"

Old Snapper slowly opened his eyes. "What do you want to know?" he asked.

"First," said the littlest turtle, "I should like to know why there is green moss on your back."

"It's because I am old," Old Snapper told him. "You will have moss on your back, too, if you live to be as old as I am. A mossy back is a very good thing, and mine has helped me to catch many a good dinner. When I lie on the bottom of the swamp with my head inside my shell, the small swamp creatures think I am a stone. When they get close enough, I stretch out my head and catch them in my jaws."

"So that's how you get your food, is it?" asked the littlest turtle.

"That's one way," Old Snapper answered. "And now if you have no more questions, go back to the cattails where you belong."

"I have another question," the littlest turtle said quickly. "Will you please tell me what is on the other side of the swamp—over there among the weeds and tall grass?"

"No," answered Old Snapper. "You will know about the other side of the swamp when you are older."

"But I want to know now," the littlest turtle said. "Could I swim over there and find out?"

"Of course not," Old Snapper answered. "You must not go while you are so small, young turtle. There are dangers in the swamp."

"Indeed there are!" said a crawfish, swimming out from under the log on which the turtles sat.

"There are a great many dangers here. Why, almost every day I meet some of them."

"But I have my shell," the littlest turtle told the crawfish. "When I pull my head and feet inside my shell, nothing can harm me."

At this, Old Snapper stretched his head far out of his shell. "Only a very young turtle would talk like that," he said crossly. "Your shell is a good thing, of course. No one else at the swamp has such a fine hard shell as we turtles have. But you must look out for danger just the same."

"Yes," cried the crawfish, "you must always look out for danger."

And then, as though frightened by his own words, the crawfish swam backward, and hid again under the log.

The young turtle was a little frightened by what he had just heard, and looked around him. The sun was still shining on the water, and the cattails still stood straight and tall. Could there really be danger in this quiet place, he wondered.

"Don't be too frightened," Old Snapper said kindly. "The crawfish has more to fear than we have, because his shell is not so hard as ours. We have our jaws, too," he went on. "We snapping turtles can bite very hard when we want to. But even with our shell and our jaws, we must always look out for danger."

"I will try to be careful," the littlest turtle said, "but I want to see the swamp—all of it. I want to see all the creatures who live here, too. I know the crawfish and the frogs already, but there must be many others."

"Yes," Old Snapper told him. "A great many different creatures live in the swamp."

"Will you tell me about them?" asked the littlest turtle.

"Not now," said the old turtle. "I am sleepy. Go away and let me have my nap. I've answered enough questions for today."

"All right," said the littlest turtle, slipping into the water. "Thank you for all you have told me."

25

The littlest turtle swam away toward the cattails, but as he went along, he thought again of the tall grass on the other side of the swamp. "I will go over and have a look at it before I go home," he thought. "I don't believe there is anyone who will harm me."

Turning about, he swam as fast as he could. Soon he began to feel hungry. He was tired, too, and now the other side of the swamp seemed very far away. "Perhaps I should go back to the cattails after all," he thought. He was about to turn back when his nose caught the exciting smell of food.

The littlest turtle went quickly under water to see what had such an exciting smell. Farther and farther down he swam until at last he came to the bottom of the swamp. There he saw a fine fat bug. It lay quite still, as though waiting to be eaten.

The littlest turtle quickly closed his jaws on the bug, but before he had time to swallow it, something happened. He felt himself pulled up from the bottom of the swamp. He was afraid, but he kept his jaws closed on the food he wanted so much.

Up, up, he was pulled, until he was out of the water and was swinging through the air toward the bank of the swamp.

Too late, the littlest turtle saw his danger. Too late, he dropped the food he was holding, and pulled his head and feet inside his shell. Instead of falling into the water, he landed on the soft bank.

"Oh, look!" said a boy's voice. "I had a turtle on my hook. See how he pulls his head and feet inside his shell!"

"Don't get your fingers too near his jaws," said the second boy. "Those turtles can bite even when they are babies."

The littlest turtle did not know what the two boys were saying, but their voices frightened him.

"I'm going to put him back in the swamp," the first boy said. "He's too young to be away from home. I don't fish for baby turtles."

As soon as the boy dropped him in the water, the littlest turtle swam quickly away. "Old Snapper was right," he thought. "There are

28

dangers here in the swamp. The next time I will listen to what he says."

He swam straight for the cattails, and had almost reached them when he felt something near him in the water. Looking around, he saw Old Snapper swimming beside him.

"What's the matter, young turtle?" Old Snapper asked. "You seem to be in a hurry."

"I have just met a danger," the littlest turtle told him. "It frightened me. I did not listen to you, Old Snapper, and I went to the other side of the swamp. But I will never do it again."

"Good!" said the old turtle. "See that you don't. The next time you may not get off so easily. And now suppose we find some food, and then go over to the log or the bank of the swamp and take a nap. You must be very tired."

The littlest turtle did not answer. He drew nearer to Old Snapper, and together they swam along through the dark-green water.

Alice Crew Gall AND *Fleming Crew*

THE LITTLE TURTLE

There was a little turtle.
He lived in a box.
He swam in a puddle.
He climbed on the rocks.

He snapped at a mosquito.
He snapped at a flea.
He snapped at a minnow.
And he snapped at me.

He caught the mosquito.
He caught the flea.
He caught the minnow.
But he didn't catch me.

Vachel Lindsay

THE BEND IN THE ROAD

Too Many Questions

Spot was a black-and-white spotted calf, and Blossom was his mother. They lived with a great many other cows in Mr. Morgan's pasture.

It was a lovely place to live. There was tall green grass for Spot to eat when he was hungry, and there was a clear cool brook for Spot to wade in on hot summer days. There was a shed where Spot could go when it rained.

But he was not a happy little calf. The cows around him seemed to like staying in the pasture, eating the tall green grass, or looking over the fence into the next field. Every evening Rusty, Mr. Morgan's dog, drove them to the barn. The next morning they were driven back again, through the barnyard, through the gate, along the road, and into the green pasture. Each day was just like the day before.

All day long, Spot asked his mother one question after another. "Where does Mr. Morgan go when he drives through the gate every morning? Why can't I go where he goes? What is there over the hill? What happens around the bend in the road?"

Poor Blossom was tired out by his questions.

"Spot, why can't you be happy like the others?" she would say. But day after day Spot asked questions which his mother could not answer. He kept asking her to let him go to see what was happening in other pastures, and she kept telling him he was too young.

32

"I'll go anyway," thought Spot. "Mother will not mind when I come back and tell her my wonderful adventures. She will be proud of me then."

One lovely day in September, Spot stood looking over the fence and down the road. He could not see very far. There was always the bend in the road, and he could not see beyond it.

That night, when the cows were driven out of the pasture, along the road, through the gate, and into the barnyard, Spot did not follow the others. Instead of going into the barnyard, he went down the barnyard road and out on the highway that ran past Mr. Morgan's house. At last he would see the world.

It was growing dark as Spot left the barnyard, so no one saw him. He felt excited as he went along. He had never been so far before. What wonderful things he might find!

Soon it became so dark that Spot could hardly see. A new and frightening thought came to him. Where would he spend the night?

Spot hurried as fast as his legs could carry him until he came to the next farm. There, in one corner of a pasture, he saw a few cows.

"M-oo-oo!" called Spot gently. "M-oo-oo!"

He waited a minute. There was no answer.

"M-oo-oo!" he tried again. "M-oo-oo!"

This time one cow came to the gate. Stretching out her neck, she asked, "Who are you and what do you want?"

Spot told her who he was. When he told her that his mother's name was Blossom, she began to ask a great many questions.

"How is your mother? I know her very well. Does Rusty still drive the cows every day? Is the grass still green?"

She went on and on, until Spot grew tired of answering. He was glad when she stopped, and he could ask a question himself.

"May I sleep here tonight?"

She told him to sleep under a big willow tree.

Spot didn't sleep very well that night. He was too excited. What adventures would he meet tomorrow? What strange pastures would he find around the next bend in the road?

He could hardly wait until daylight to see what this pasture looked like. But when it was light, he could hardly believe his eyes. Here was a green field, and a brook with willow trees. A wooden fence ran around it all. It was no nicer than the home pasture. In fact, he didn't think the grass was so good.

Soon he said good-by to his new friends and started down the highway again.

All the morning he went along the road. Whenever he heard someone coming, he went up on the bank and ate a little grass, just as if he belonged there. Each time he came to a bend in the road, he hurried around it, hoping that he would find something different. Each time, the pasture that he saw might have been the one he had left.

"Is the whole world like this?" cried Spot, sadly. "Are all the pastures like my own? I might just as well have stayed at home if I am never going to see anything different."

Late in the afternoon Spot heard a noise up the road. Soon some cows, spotted black and white like himself, came into sight. When they saw him, a few of them ran up on the bank where he was.

"Where are you going in such a hurry?" asked Spot.

"To the County Fair," answered the cows.

"County Fair?" said Spot. "What is that?"

A friendly cow said, "The County Fair is a place where cows and sheep and pigs and other animals are taken each year. If you are fine and healthy, and if your father and mother and your grandfather and grandmother were fine and healthy, you may get a blue ribbon."

At last here was something different.

"Let me come with you," said Spot. "Your driver will think that I belong to you." So Spot started on his way to the County Fair.

The cows were driven along the road until at last they began to meet so many people that Spot was surprised.

"What is this?" he asked. "Why are there so many people?"

"This is the city," said the cows. "In a city a great many people live close together. They live so close together that there is no room for cows and sheep and horses."

Soon the cows were driven in through a big gate, along another road, past some large buildings, and then into a long shed.

"Here we are," said the cows. "Now we shall lead easy lives for a week. All we have to do is to stay in clean stalls where we have soft beds of straw. When people come along to look at us, we try to look our best."

Spot was put into a pen with some other calves and he found it as nice as the cows had said. People passed by and looked at him. He heard them say, "My, what a pretty calf!"

38

Spot was so sure they were talking about him that he felt very proud.

Several days passed. One morning three men came along with papers in their hands.

One man looked at his paper and then at Spot and said, "Hello, what's this! This calf isn't put down on Mr. Green's paper. Mr. Green must have forgotten him."

"That is strange," answered the other man. "I can't find him on my paper, either. He's a fine-looking little fellow, too. He should get a ribbon. We must ask Mr. Green about him."

Soon four excited men hurried up to Spot's pen. Spot was surprised to see that one of them was Mr. Morgan.

"That's Spot, sure enough," said Mr. Morgan. "See the white spot on his ear? I wonder how he got here." Turning to Spot, he said, "Spot, where did you come from? I thought I had lost you. I was going to bring you here myself."

Spot certainly was a happy calf that day. He knew now that he would get back to his mother all right. He was already tired of the County Fair. He wanted his cool brook to wade in, and his mother to keep him warm at night.

40

One more thing made Spot happy that day.
The men who had first found him came back and
tied a blue ribbon on him. One of them said to
Mr. Morgan, "I see that your calf got a blue
ribbon. He's a fine fellow."

The next day Mr. Morgan took Spot home.
He didn't have to walk all those miles this time.
He was carried home in a big truck. In no time
at all, he was back in Mr. Morgan's pasture,
telling his adventures to his mother. His mother
was not very cross. She was glad to see him and
know that he was all right.

Now, when Spot stands in his pasture with the cows, and looks far off down the road, he is not unhappy. He does not worry his mother with questions. He does not wonder any more what is happening around the bend in the road. He knows. Around the bend in the road are pastures just like his own, and at the end of the road is a County Fair, where he will go again next year.

Phyllis Fenner

COUNTY FAIR DAY

Oh, the County Fair! The County Fair!
Cattle and pigs and a dancing bear!
And gypsies and merry-go-rounds and kegs
Of cream and butter and new-laid eggs;
And fortune tellers and bright balloons
Bobbing like little colored moons!

Rachel Field

THEY WANTED A PET

KITTENS' QUESTIONNAIRE

I met four young and handsome kits,
In black fur coats and velvet mitts.

They asked me many questions: "Why
Do mice run fast and robins fly?

"Where do balls roll? Why should a feather
Do such strange tricks in windy weather?

"What makes a big dog rush about?
What makes a bowl of cream give out?

"Why does our mother never fail
To box us when we pat her tail?

"Oh, tell us, tell us, if you can, sir!"
I didn't know a single answer.

Nancy Byrd Turner

SNEAKERS

That Rapscallion Cat

Once there was a little fat cat, and his name was Sneakers. His mother called him Sneakers because he had four white paws and the rest of him was black. Her other little kittens were black all over.

46

When his mother saw Sneakers lying on his back, waving his four white paws in the air, she thought he must have gone walking in her dish of milk while she was taking a nap. She picked him out of her pile of kittens by his neck, and she held him between her two front paws, and tried to clean the milk off his little feet, and make them black like all her other kittens' feet. She licked and she licked, and she purred and she purred, but still he had four white paws.

Just then she saw a little boy running toward her. It was the first warm day in the year, and he had on a pair of clean white sneakers.

The mother cat looked at the little boy's sneakers, and she looked at the little kitten with his four white paws. She blinked at the little boy's sneakers, and she blinked at her kitten with his four white paws. Then she purred and she purred and she purred, and the little kitten was called Sneakers from then on.

Now this Sneakers was a rapscallion cat. While the other kittens stayed in the box until they grew up, Sneakers was out of the box even before his eyes were open. When he grew up enough, he went running after little black bugs across the ground.

He went pounce, pounce, pounce, all day long, and then he went pounce into his bed at night. Tucking his little white paws under him into a warm fur ball, he went to sleep.

His mother always knew that no matter how much he went pouncing off, he would always come pouncing back, so she did not worry about him. But she did think over and over again, "By my nose and whiskers, this is a funny little cat!"

48

One day his mother licked his little face, and she said to him, "Now, Sneakers, my kitten, my little fur cat, away you go! You are to live in the house with the little boy. You will catch the mice, and make the little boy laugh, but you must never knock anything off the tables. I am a barn cat, and my home is in the barn here in the hay. But you will be a house cat, and will sleep before the fire and only come out here in the daytime. Now off you go to the house, and keep your little paws clean as the milk that you drink every morning."

So Sneakers went to live in the big house and be the little boy's kitten. At first it seemed very quiet in the house at night. In the barn, the horses were always moving around in their stalls, and the mice were squeaking in the hay.

Then at table one day, the little boy knocked over a plate of peaches. They rolled all over the floor in every direction—little round peaches rolling away.

49

"My, but I'm glad this happened," thought the funny little kitten, as he went pounce on one of the peaches. "I wish that lots of things would come rolling all over the floor."

Everyone laughed so hard at Sneakers that they forgot who knocked the peaches off the table. The little boy laughed, too.

One afternoon the cook came back from town all dressed up in a fine new hat—a fine new hat with red feathers on it. She met Sneakers in the kitchen.

"Where are you going, you little Sneaker cat?"

"Just prowling around—prowling around." Sneakers blinked his bright yellow eyes.

Just then the wind came blowing in the kitchen door. It blew the cook's hat, with all its red feathers, off onto the floor.

Pounce! went Sneakers. Pounce on the feathers and the fine new hat. He pushed it across the floor.

"Oh, Sneakers, you kitten, you rapscallion cat! Give me back my fine new hat!"

But Sneakers was having fun, and the cook moved very slowly. He knocked the hat with his milk-white paw and thought, "My, but I am glad this happened!" And he pushed the hat under the table.

The cook had to run all over the kitchen after him before she could get her hat. She put it back on top of her head, and stood there. Sneakers just sat and licked his milk-white paw.

"Oh, Sneakers," said the cook, "the minute I saw you I knew that you were a rapscallion cat."

SNEAKERS COMES TO TOWN

Sneakers went prowling around and prowling around all summer on his sneaker white paws, and he grew from a kitten to a little cat. He was still the little boy's cat, and he was still a rapscallion cat.

When the little boy caught a fish in the river and pulled it up on the bank, pounce went Sneakers on the fish. When the cook's feet went walking

by one of Sneakers' hiding places, pounce went
Sneakers on the cook's feet. He was a rapscallion
cat. But the little boy loved him, and he was
the little boy's cat.

Then, one day at the end of summer, the whole
house packed up to go to town for the winter.
The cook packed her big hat with the red feathers.
The little boy's mother packed all the straw hats
and all the silver knives and forks and spoons.

She packed all the little boy's sneakers and socks.
She packed all his summer clothes and his toys.
The little boy's father packed his fishing rods and
all his clothes. Then they all got into the big car
with all the suitcases to drive to town.

The little boy was very sad. Sneakers was not
to go with them. His mother said the city was
no place for an animal, and his father said that
all animals belonged in the country. Sneakers
would have to stay with the farmer in the next
house and wait all winter for the little boy to
come back. Just before the car drove off, the
little boy jumped out to tell Sneakers good-by.
He called Sneakers, but the little cat didn't come.

54

He looked all through the house, but Sneakers wasn't there.

He looked in the cellar, he looked in the barn, and he looked in the field behind the barn. No Sneakers.

So the little boy just called out across the field, "Good-by, my Sneakers, my rapscallion cat."

Then he went back to the car. The car drove off to the city, and no one saw Sneakers to tell him good-by.

When they got to the city, they drove to the little boy's city house. It had a very small garden in front of it behind a high iron fence. The garden was the size of a very small rug. It was not even big enough to run in without bumping into the big iron fence.

The little boy's mother and his father and the cook went into the house. The cook unpacked her hat. His mother unpacked the silver knives and forks and spoons. His father unpacked the fishing rods.

Then his mother opened the suitcases to unpack some clothes. First she opened the suitcase with the little boy's toys in it. Some toys and sticks fell all over the floor.

Then the little boy's mother opened the suitcase with his father's clothes. She unpacked them and hung them up in the closet. Then she opened her own suitcase and hung up all her dresses.

Then she opened the little boy's suitcase. And—wait! What in the world? Out jumped a little black ball of fur and jumped up on the bed. It was Sneakers. Sneakers was purring and purring, and stretching out his little white paws. He mewed just once when the little boy ran up to him.

"Oh, that Sneakers, that rapscallion cat!" said the little boy's mother. "How in the world did he get in that suitcase?"

"He must have fallen asleep there and we didn't see him when we closed the suitcase. That bad little cat!" The little boy's father was smiling.

The little boy didn't say anything. He just

patted Sneakers, and Sneakers purred and purred and purred.

"What will we ever do in the city with a rapscallion cat!" said the little boy's mother. "We will have to send him back to the country when the car goes back."

"No," said the little boy's father. "If he has come this far all by himself, let him stay."

So the little cat stayed in the city with the little boy, and they played in the garden with the high iron fence.

Margaret Wise Brown

MICE

I think mice
Are rather nice.

Their tails are long,
Their faces small,
They haven't any
Chins at all.
Their ears are pink,
Their teeth are white,
They run about
The house at night.
They nibble things
They shouldn't touch,
And no one seems
To like them much.

But I think mice
Are nice.

Rose Fyleman

JIM JUMPER

A Funny Mouse

Jim Jumper lived in New York City. He was a white mouse with round ears, a long tail, and bright black eyes. Jim Jumper was a pet mouse, so he couldn't run across the floor, hide under chairs, and slip into a hole when he heard someone coming. He couldn't slip into the kitchen after all the family were asleep, to see if there was any food left around, and perhaps find something to eat. Since Jim Jumper was a pet mouse, he had to live in a cage.

It was a pretty cage. It looked something like a bird cage. There was fresh sawdust on the floor. There was a little dish for food, and another little dish for water.

Jim Jumper belonged to a little boy named Christopher, who took good care of him and gave him food and water every day. Christopher laughed to see the mouse run round and round. But Jim Jumper wanted to be free. He wanted to find some other mice to play with. He was lonely, even though the little boy was good to him.

Jim Jumper had not been lonely in the pet shop. His mother and all his brothers and sisters had been there. When he wanted to play, there was always someone to play with him. When he felt sleepy, he could go to sleep with the other little mice. Their fur was soft and warm. Jim Jumper's cage, where he slept now, was clean and nice, but he often wished for the feeling of fur again, just as he wished to be free.

One day Christopher had to stay home from school. It was a rainy day, and he had a little cold. Christopher was glad at first that he could

stay at home and play all day. He played with his train, until he was tired of that. Then he played with his cars. Then he drew pictures.

By the middle of the morning, Christopher was tired of playing with his toys. He came to watch Jim Jumper in his cage. Jim Jumper was so happy to have Christopher watch him that he did all his tricks. He rolled over. He stood on his hind legs with his little paws against the door of the cage.

"Mother," said Christopher. "Jim is such a good pet mouse. I am sure he wouldn't run away. May I take him out of the cage and play with him?"

Christopher's mother was in the other room, talking over the telephone. She didn't hear him.

"She didn't say 'no'," thought Christopher. So he opened the door of the cage, and caught Jim Jumper in his two hands.

What a little thing he was! Why should anyone ever be afraid of a mouse? Christopher laughed as Jim ran up his arm and over his shoulder. He caught him as he was about to run inside a pocket, and put him on the floor. And there the mouse was when Christopher's mother finished telephoning and came into the room.

"Christopher!" said his mother. "Did I say you might take the mouse out of the cage?"

"No," said Christopher. "But you didn't tell me not to. And he is so funny, Mother. Look!"

Christopher's mother looked at Jim Jumper. She did think that he was funny, as he turned his head this way and that and wrinkled his little nose. He was having a fine time. He was free, for a little while. If only he could get away through an open door, and find some other mice to play with!

62

"He seems to be looking for something," said Christopher. "What do you suppose it is?"

"I don't know," said his mother. "But you must put him back in the cage now, Christopher. There is the telephone again."

Christopher's mother left the room and shut the door behind her. Christopher was sure that Jim Jumper could not get away, so he didn't put him back in the cage. Christopher watched him for a while. Then he forgot all about him.

Jim Jumper didn't care. Now was the time to run away. He ran quietly, as mice do, to the door. The door was shut tight. Then he ran up chair legs and across tables. He ran across the bed, and in and out among the pillows. A fur coat was thrown over one end of the bed. The soft fur made Jim Jumper think of his mother and his brothers and his sisters. He crawled right up inside one sleeve and went to sleep.

GOING TO MARKET

Later in the day Christopher's mother said, "The sun is out now, and I have some shopping to do. Your cold is so much better that you may come to market with me. I need help to carry the bundles home."

"Oh, yes," said Christopher, for he liked to go to the market. He put his toys away and ran to get his coat and hat.

The market near Christopher's house was a wonderful place. There were boxes of vegetables and boxes of fruit all around. The market was full of people, men with aprons on, and women with handkerchiefs over their heads. These were the market people, but there were many shoppers, too, like Christopher and his mother.

Christopher was holding a bag of apples and a box of figs, while his mother was looking in her purse for some money. All at once she gave a little jump.

"Oh!" she cried. "There's something in my sleeve!"

Jim Jumper had just waked up.

"What's the matter, Mother?" asked Christopher, while the market-man stared.

"Oh-h-h!" said his mother again.

Jim Jumper was tired of being inside the sleeve of a fur coat, and he had started to find his way out. He was running down her arm!

Christopher dropped the apples and the figs.

65

His mother's purse fell to the floor of the market as the little white mouse ran away to freedom.

"Oh, that's Jim Jumper!" cried Christopher. "Catch him, catch him!"

Jim Jumper did not wait to be caught. A market was a better place for a mouse than a cage. It was better than a pet shop. With a wrinkle of his nose, and a wave of his tail, Jim Jumper ran behind a box of oranges and hid.

Christopher never saw Jim Jumper again. He may be living in the market still. Or perhaps he has moved into a house with a mouse-hole, and a kitchen with good things to eat in it. Anyway, he is a free mouse, and there are many other free mice for him to play with in the city.

Eleanor Frances Lattimore

THEY WANTED A HORSE

Erik and Elmer

Erik and Elmer wanted a horse. They wanted a horse more than anything else in the world.

They wanted it more than lollipops or ice cream. They wanted it more than an afternoon at the circus. That is how much they wanted a horse.

"If we just had a horse," said Erik.

"We could ride it all around the farm and over to the lake when we go swimming," said Elmer.

"Let's buy a horse," said Erik.

"Let's save all our money and buy a horse," said Elmer. "Let's do that."

So all spring and summer they saved their money, for they wanted a horse more than anything else in the world. When their mother gave Erik five cents for weeding the garden, he put it in the toe of an old sock and hid it under the bed where he and Elmer slept. When their father gave Elmer five cents for feeding the chickens, Elmer put it in the old sock and hid the sock again. When the hired man gave them a dime for watching the horses while he took a nap under the apple tree, they carried the dime home and tucked it into their hiding place. They saved and saved and saved. That is how much Erik and Elmer wanted a horse.

Every Saturday morning they would take out the old sock and shake it to see how much it jingled. Every Saturday the jingling was louder. At first the jingling had been so small that it seemed as if their money would buy a horse no bigger than a kitten. But now the noise was loud and cheerful.

"That sounds like a fine big horse—almost," said Erik.

"Yes," said Elmer. "In a little while we can buy a good big horse."

Every week the sock grew heavier, just as they had hoped. Erik sold some eggs his hen had laid. Elmer picked some berries and sold them. Their father gave them money to spend in town on Saturday, and they saved that, too. The jingling grew louder and louder. Uncle Carl visited them from the city, and he gave them each a dollar bill. He wanted them to have that horse, too.

But the dollar bills did not make any noise in the old sock. So the next Saturday night, when the family went to town, they changed the bills into fifty-cent pieces. The heavy silver pieces would make a fine noise in the sock.

They did make a fine noise. They made a loud ringing in the old sock. They made so loud a ringing and jingling that Erik and Elmer looked at each other and grinned.

The next morning at breakfast Erik and Elmer showed the old sock to their father.

"How big a horse would this money buy?" asked Erik.

"It sounds like a big horse to me," said Elmer, jingling the sock.

Their father took the sock and shook it.

"Yes, it sounds good and loud," he said.

"It will be a good big horse," said their mother.

"Oh, yes," said the hired man.

"How much money is it?" asked their father.

"Oh, we never counted it," said Erik.

"But we can count it now," said Elmer, as he emptied the money out on the table.

Erik and Elmer counted the money. Their father and their mother helped them and the hired man helped, too. They all counted out loud. It took a long time.

At last they found the answer. It was fourteen dollars and sixty-two cents.

"Well, well!" said their father. "Fourteen dollars and sixty-two cents is a lot of money!"

"Is it enough for a horse?" Erik asked.

"Almost enough for some kind of horse," said their father. "Shall we make it fifteen dollars even?"

"Yes," said the hired man. "Here are three cents toward it."

"And here is a dime," said their mother.

"And here is a quarter," said their father. "Now it's fifteen dollars even."

"Oh, thanks," said Erik and Elmer together.

"Will that buy a real horse?" Erik asked.

"Yes," said their father. "But it won't be a race horse, you understand."

"But a horse!" said Erik and Elmer.

"Oh, yes," said their father. "On Saturday night, when we go to town, we will look around for one."

Erik and Elmer picked up the money and tucked it back into the old sock.

72

Every night that week they dreamed about the new horse. Every morning they jingled the sockful of money.

"At last," they said to each other. "At last we have money enough to buy a real horse to ride everywhere we please. We'll buy him next Saturday night!"

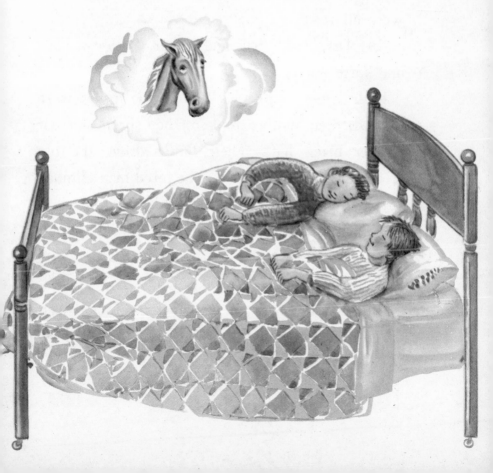

It was Saturday. As soon as supper was over, Erik and Elmer were going into town with their father and their mother.

They had wet their hair and brushed it to make it lie down flat. They had put on their best blue shirts and their new overalls. They were all ready to go.

"At last," said Erik and Elmer, "we can have our horse!"

Right after supper, as soon as the dishes were washed, their mother took off her apron and put on her black hat. Their father drove the old green car out of the barn. The hired man climbed into the back seat. Erik and Elmer climbed in beside him with the sockful of money held carefully between them.

Away they went toward town.

Erik and Elmer were watching the money bag so closely that they did not see the cornfields they were passing, nor the banks of the river. They did not see a thing but the money bag.

At last they came to Main Street and found a place to leave the car. All the farmers from miles around had come to town with their families for Saturday night.

"One of them should have a horse to sell," said Erik.

"One of them will have a horse," said Elmer. "I'm sure of that."

Their mother went into the ten-cent store to buy some things for the kitchen, and the hired man went into the market to visit with his friends. Erik and Elmer and their father walked along Main Street looking for someone with a horse to sell.

"There's Carl Johnson. He might know of one," said their father.

But Carl Johnson shook his head from side to side and said no, he just did not know of a horse for sale.

They asked one person, and another, and another. No one had a horse to sell.

"You just wait," their father said to Erik and Elmer. "There are plenty of people to ask yet."

They walked on down Main Street to the last corner, where the drug store was. Leaning against the doorpost of the drug store was old Axel Peterson.

"Hello," he called to Erik and Elmer and their father. "How are you?"

"Oh, we are fine. Just a little tired out, looking for a horse."

"Want to buy a horse?" asked Axel.

"Well, a sort of horse," said the boys' father. "Not much of a horse, you know. A good safe horse."

"The horse is for us," said Elmer.

"We have all this money," said Erik, shaking the sock.

"I have a horse I could sell you," said Axel Peterson. "Not a race horse, you understand."

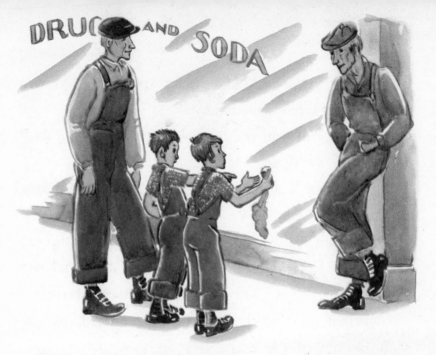

"We have all this money," said Erik, shaking the sock.

"It's fifteen dollars even," said Elmer. "We saved it all for a horse."

Old Axel shut one eye and then he shut the other eye.

"Well," said Axel. "That's a bargain. You can have my old horse. For fifteen dollars you can have her forever. She's an old horse, remember. No race horse, but fine for two boys."

"Oh," said Erik and Elmer together. "Where is she? Here's the money."

"Wait till you see her. Maybe she won't do."

"Oh, she'll do," said Erik.

"Yes, she'll do," said Elmer. "We want to buy her tonight."

As soon as their mother had finished her shopping, she and Erik and Elmer and their father and the hired man drove out to Axel Peterson's farm.

When they reached his farm, Axel led the old horse out of the barn.

"Just an old horse, as you can see," said Axel.

"Mmmm," said their father. "A sort of horse. But she looks kind."

"Oh, yes! She's kind. She's very kind. She'll never run away."

Erik and Elmer were grinning. She was a wonderful horse! She was a white horse. And she had a long white tail.

"Here's the money," said Erik and Elmer. "Let's start home."

"Now if that horse does not please, let me know," said Axel.

"Oh, she'll do!" cried Elmer.

"She'll do!" cried Erik. "Let's start home."

So old Axel tied the rope to the back of the old green car.

"Her name is Kristie," said Axel. "Good Old Kristie, I always call her."

Slowly the green car started along the road. Slowly, pulling back against the rope, Good Old Kristie followed after. Erik and Elmer leaned over the back of the seat to be sure that nothing happened to her. Nothing did.

They were soon at home. Erik and Elmer untied Kristie from the car and led her carefully into a stall in the barn. They fixed some straw for a bed and gave her oats and hay to eat. They patted her thin sides. They were very happy. Both wanted to sit up all night with Kristie, but their mother said, "No."

"Half a night each, then," said Erik and Elmer.

"No," said their father. "Kristie can take care of herself."

So Erik and Elmer gave her a last pat and went to bed. They had their new horse at last. She was their very own. They hoped the night would not be too long.

Going for a Ride

Early in the morning, before the sun was up, Erik and Elmer got up. They put on their shirts and overalls. They did not stop to comb their hair. They crept downstairs and hurried to the barn.

It was very dark inside but they knew where to find their new horse Kristie.

Kristie neighed when they came into her stall.

81

"See, she knows us," said Erik.

"Of course she does," said Elmer. "She belongs to us."

They led Good Old Kristie out into the early morning light. How white she would look after she was cleaned up a bit!

"I'll get a rag and some soft soap," said Erik.

"And I'll get some water," said Elmer.

They tied Kristie to the fence and they washed and washed her until she was clean. They braided her tail to make it wave, and they braided her bangs to keep the hair out of her eyes. Kristie was good and did not say a word.

Erik and Elmer were working so hard that they forgot all about breakfast until their mother called them.

They ate all their breakfast in the time they should have used to eat half of it.

"Now we're going for a ride," said Erik.

"We're going down to the lake for a swim," said Elmer.

82

Erik and Elmer and their father and their mother went out and stood around Good Old Kristie. The hired man came out, too, and sat on the fence. The horse stood shining in the sun.

Erik brought a box from the barn and put it down beside her. He and Elmer stood on the box and their father helped them climb onto Kristie's back. Erik sat in front and held the rope in his hands. Elmer sat behind and held fast to Erik's overalls.

"Good-by. Here we go," they cried.

"Gid-ap, Kristie, gid-ap," they called together. But Kristie did not move.

"Gid-ap!" they called and swung their bare heels against her sides.

Kristie did not move. She tossed her head and stood right where she was.

"I'll get some hay," said their father.

He brought some hay and held it out in front of Kristie.

"Come, girl, come on," he said.

Kristie stretched out her long thin neck and took the hay. She chewed it carefully, but she did not move.

"I'll get some sugar," said their mother. "That will work." She ran into the kitchen and came out again with two lumps of sugar in her hand.

"Come, Good Old Kristie," she called, standing just out of Kristie's reach. "Come on."

Kristie took a step forward and took the sugar, but she would not move another inch.

"It's no use," said their father. "We'll have to ask Axel Peterson what is the matter when we go to town next Saturday night. She was his horse for a long time. He will know what is the matter."

Erik and Elmer did not know how they could wait until Saturday night. Six days were so long. But each day they fed Good Old Kristie oats and hay. They took her out so that she could sun herself every morning. They gave her a clean bed of straw every night.

Kristie was very fond of Erik and Elmer. She neighed when they came into the barn, and she hunted for lumps of sugar in their pockets. But she would not take them for a ride.

At last Saturday night came. Erik and Elmer were all dressed up in their best blue shirts and new overalls. As soon as the supper dishes were washed, they started on their way.

Erik and Elmer were in a great hurry to reach Main Street, and their father drove as fast as he could. At last they stopped at the corner where the drug store was. Old Axel Peterson was leaning against the doorpost.

"Hello, there," he called to Erik and Elmer. "How is Good Old Kristie?"

"She's fine," said Erik.

"She's all washed and clean," said Elmer.

"But she won't go," they said together.

"She won't go?" asked Axel Peterson, his eyes big with surprise. "She won't go!"

"No," said Erik and Elmer.

"Well," said Axel, shutting one eye. "Well, just think of that," he said, shutting the other eye.

"What can we do?" asked Erik and Elmer.

"Do you give her plenty of hay and a good bed?" he asked.

"Oh, yes," said Erik.

"And sugar lumps, too," said Elmer.

"And she won't go?" asked Axel. "Did you by any chance leave off her hat?"

"Her hat?" said Erik.

"She has no hat," said Elmer.

"There! Did I forget to give you her hat? She always wears a hat. Winter and summer she wears a hat. Of course she won't go if she isn't wearing her hat!"

"Wearing her hat?" cried Erik.

"Her hat?" cried Elmer. "Then let's get her hat right away. We want to go swimming."

They went home with Axel Peterson. They followed along after his little old black car. When they reached his farm, he went into the barn and brought out an old straw hat. There were two holes for ears to go through. It was easy to see it was a horse's hat.

"Now she'll go. You watch," said Axel Peterson. "Put on her hat and Good Old Kristie will go as fast as you please."

"Oh, thank you," said Erik and Elmer together.

They took the old straw hat and held it carefully on their knees. They were grinning all the way home.

88

Try Again

The next morning, as soon as the sun was up, Erik and Elmer jumped out of bed and went to the barn. They could hear Kristie neighing.

"She likes us," said Erik.

"But just wait until she sees her old hat," said Elmer.

Erik took the hat down from the nail where they had hung it the night before. Then he and Elmer went into Kristie's stall. Erik held the hat, and Elmer held Kristie. Erik put the hat on her head and pulled her ears through the holes. Elmer tied the strings under her chin. Kristie neighed loudly and tossed her head.

"Now she'll go," they said. "Let's hurry and eat breakfast."

They ate all their breakfast in the time that they should have taken to eat one quarter of it.

"Now that she has her old hat again, she will go and we will ride her to the lake and go in swimming."

Erik and Elmer and their father and their mother went out and stood around Good Old Kristie. Their mother gave her three lumps of sugar. The hired man came too, and sat on the fence.

Old Kristie was looking very gay and ready to step off at any moment. Her ears stood straight up through the holes in the hat. Her braided bangs hung down over her nose. Her two eyes shone.

Erik brought a box from the barn and put it down beside her. He and Elmer stood on the box, and their father pushed them up on Kristie's back.

"Look out!" they cried. "Here we go!"

Kristie shook herself so that Erik and Elmer could hardly stay on her back. Then she turned and started to run. She ran across the barnyard as fast as she could run. Then she stopped suddenly, and spread out her front feet on her two thin legs.

Erik and Elmer yelled loudly. As Kristie stopped, they shot over her head and over her straw hat down onto the ground.

Kristie tossed her head. Erik picked himself up from the ground, rubbing his back. Elmer picked himself up, rubbing his two knees.

"Well, I never!" said their father and their mother and the hired man. "Well, I never!"

"What can be the matter now?" said their father, as he patted Kristie's nose.

They tried to think of everything.

"She has plenty of food," said Erik.

"And a good bed," said Elmer.

"And her sugar," said their mother.

"And she's wearing her hat," called the hired man from the fence where he was sitting.

Erik went up to Kristie and fixed her hat. Elmer tied the strings again under her chin. Their mother brought three more lumps of sugar. While Kristie was eating the sugar, their father helped Erik up on her back.

92

"Try it again, just one of you," he said. "Maybe she does not like two."

Erik shook the rope and patted her sides with his bare feet.

"Gid-ap, Kristie," he said politely.

Kristie did not look happy. She shook herself as hard as she could. Then she jumped forward, stopped suddenly, and leaned back on her four thin legs. In one second Erik flew from her back and over her head to the ground.

Kristie snorted and shook her head.

"Let me try," said Elmer. "Maybe she'll like me better."

His father helped Elmer up on to Kristie's back.

"Gid-ap, please," Elmer said softly.

Kristie was looking crosser than ever. She kicked up her hind legs, bent down her long thin neck, and sent Elmer flying through the air.

"Well, I never!" said the boys' father and mother and the hired man.

"She goes all right," said Erik.

"Yes, at least she goes," said Elmer as he picked himself up and shook himself like a puppy.

"What can be the matter with her?" said their father. "We'll have to wait until we go to town next Saturday night and ask Old Axel Peterson."

Erik and Elmer did not know how they could wait again until Saturday night. Six days were so long. But at last Saturday night came. Right after supper the whole family and the hired man climbed into the little old green car and drove to town. At the corner drug store on Main Street they found old Axel Peterson.

"Hello," he called. "How does she go?"

"Oh, fine," said Erik.

"But she won't let us stay on her back!" said Elmer.

"You didn't try to ride her?" said Axel Peterson.

"Oh, can't we ride her at all?" asked Erik and Elmer.

"Why, no," said Axel. "Of course she won't let you ride her. She'll never let you ride her. Just hitch her up to a buggy and she'll go. Good Old Kristie!"

"But we have no buggy," said Erik and Elmer.

95

"Well, I have an old buggy and some harness. I'll give them to you. The buggy is not much to look at, you understand. But I guess it will do. Hitch her to that and watch her go."

So they went home with Axel Peterson. He fastened the buggy to the back of the old green car. They pulled it home to their own farm and left it standing in the barnyard.

The next morning Erik and Elmer ate their breakfast so fast that they were through almost as soon as they began. They ran out to the barn

to their good horse Kristie. They led her out of her stall and rubbed her down. They combed her tail and braided her bangs so that the hair would not blow in her eyes. They put on her straw hat and pulled her ears through the holes. They tied the hat-strings under her chin.

"Today we are going swimming," said Erik.

"Just watch us go," said Elmer.

Their father came out and helped them harness Kristie and hitch her to the old buggy.

Their mother came out with five lumps of sugar and the hired man came out, too, and sat on the fence. Erik and Elmer climbed up to the seat of the buggy. Kristie looked happy.

"Gid-ap," said Erik, pulling gently on the reins.

"Gid-ap," said Elmer politely.

Their father stood by the gate holding his breath. He was waiting to see if Kristie would really go. Their mother stood beside him holding her breath. The hired man sat on the fence and held his breath, too.

Kristie stretched out her long thin neck. She stepped out with her four thin legs and walked quickly across the barnyard and through the gate.

"Good-by," called Erik.

"Good-by," called Elmer. "We'll be back for dinner."

"Just look at us go!" said Erik.

"I can hardly believe it," said Elmer.

Kristie stepped off along the road. She did not stop. She went just as a good horse should go, along the road toward the lake.

"Isn't this wonderful!" said Erik.

"Good Old Kristie," said Elmer.

"Old Axel Peterson was right. She's a fine old horse," they said together.

Erik and Elmer grinned all the way to the lake. They grinned all the time they were in swimming. If you did things the way that Kristie wanted them done, it was easy!

Emma Brock

ON THE WAY

RUNAWAY SONG

Hurray, hurray! Some summer day
I'll get on a horse and gallop away
  a-gallop, a-jallop
  away on a spree
Over the bridge, down to the sea!

Hurray, hurray! Some summer day
I'll get on a ship and rollick away
  a-rollick, a-frollick
  a jolly tar tune
Over the waves to Cameroon!

Hurray, hurray! Some summer day
I'll get on a plane and zoom up high
  a-soaring, a-roaring
  way up in the clear
Over the clouds and back to here!

Mark Sawyer

MR. TIMOTHY'S BOAT YARD

MORNING

Pull! Pull! Pull on the long oars! Michael rowed his boat up Little Clam Bay. He watched people fishing along the shore. They were catching little silver fish called snappers. Michael liked to watch things happen.

Michael tied his boat to the long dock at Mr. Timothy's boat yard. He liked to come here. There was always something to watch, for Mr. Timothy's boat yard was a busy place.

On the shore, he saw sailboats, shining with fresh coats of paint. He saw others with black engines waiting to be mended.

Michael ran between the boats to a man who was stirring some white paint in a big paint pot.

"Hello, Mr. Dan! Is it easy to do that?" asked Michael.

"Try it and see," Mr. Dan answered.

Michael tried it. He tried to stir it as fast as Mr. Dan had. All of a sudden his hand slipped. So did Michael! Bump! His knees went right against the fresh paint on the boat.

"Ho, ho!" laughed Mr. Dan. "Here, take this rag and rub the paint off your legs."

Michael rubbed.

"Is Mr. Timothy in the shop?" he asked.

"Yes, I think he's working on that new sailboat," answered Mr. Dan.

Off went Michael to find Mr. Timothy. It seemed dark when he looked into the shop. All that Michael could see was sawdust whirling everywhere. He closed his eyes and opened them again. Then he could see someone working at a motor.

"Mr. Timothy!" called Michael.

"Z-z-z-z!" answered the motor.

"Mr. Timothy!" Michael shouted. But the motor was making so much noise that still Mr. Timothy did not hear him.

Suddenly Mr. Timothy saw a pair of small bare legs. They were too close to the motor. Z-z-z-z-z! Mr. Timothy turned off the motor. Z-z--z---z----. The noise stopped.

"Get out of the way, there!" said Mr. Timothy. In the sudden quiet his voice sounded very loud. "Oh, it's you, Michael!"

Mr. Timothy sounded angry, but his blue eyes were kind and smiling.

"I just wanted to see you cut that board," Michael said.

"Well, I am glad I happened to see you before you came any closer," said Mr. Timothy.

"I'm going to build boats when I grow up," Michael told Mr. Timothy. "That's why I was watching you."

"How would you like to build a boat right now?" asked Mr. Timothy.

"Oh, may I? Really?"

"Right this very minute!" he said, laughing. "Come along!" He led Michael over to the other side of the shop.

"You may use any of this wood," Mr. Timothy told Michael, pulling out a pile of boards and round sticks.

"Now let me see. You'll need a saw. Here's one. And you'll need a hammer and some nails."

He gave Michael a hammer and opened a drawer full of nails.

"May I have a drill, too?" asked Michael.

"Yes, indeed. This one will be the right size. If you need help, just stay here and pound on this box with your hammer. I can hear you above the sound of my motor." Then Mr. Timothy went back to work and left Michael to start building his boat.

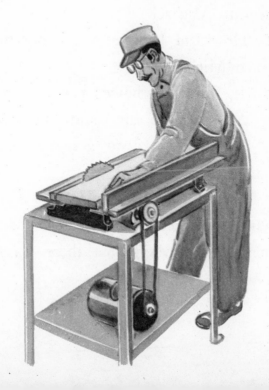

Michael sawed one end of a board so that it was pointed. Then he sawed off two round sticks. He drilled a hole near the pointed end of the board and fitted the longer stick into it. That was the mast. Michael did not know what to do next. He didn't know how to fasten the boom to the mast.

Bang! Bang! He pounded the box with the hammer.

At last Mr. Timothy heard him. His motor went Z-z--z--- and stopped. Mr. Timothy came over to Michael.

"How can I fasten the boom to the mast?" asked Michael.

Mr. Timothy showed him how to do it.

"Now for the sail," said Michael.

"You will have to get the sail," said Mr. Timothy.

Michael looked and looked all around the shop. Michael looked in corners and under boxes. He hunted everywhere, but there wasn't any cloth

that he could use for his sail. He found plenty
of dirty rags covered with paint. He found one
rag covered with green paint.

"I know!" decided Michael. "First I will
paint my boat green."

Michael picked up his little boat and ran outdoors.
There was Mr. Dan still painting. He was painting
the sailboat a beautiful green.

"Mr. Dan!" called Michael. "Look at my
boat!"

"Where? What has happened to it?" asked
Mr. Dan. He looked at Michael's rowboat. There
it was, tied up at the dock, just as Michael had
left it.

"I mean this boat," cried Michael. "Look!
Here!" He held out the little boat that he had
made.

"Well, well! That's a fine boat!"

"I want to paint it green. May I use your brush for a minute?" asked Michael.

"All right," said Mr. Dan. "Put your boat right on that box."

"Thanks!" said Michael.

With the big soft brush Michael painted the little boat very quickly. Then he put the brush back across the top of the can.

"There! She's all finished!" he cried.

"If you leave it there until after lunch, it will have time to dry," said Mr. Dan.

At that moment, Mr. Timothy came out of the big shed.

"I need to rest before lunch," he said, and started to sit down on the box.

"Watch out!" shouted both Michael and Mr. Dan together.

"Oh! Oh!" cried out Mr. Timothy, jumping up quickly.

Michael was afraid to look at his little boat.

108

"Which was hurt more?" asked Mr. Dan.

"I was!" said Mr. Timothy, making a face. "It's lucky the mast was not broken."

A whistle blew.

"Twelve o'clock," said Mr. Dan.

"I'll have to hurry home!" said Michael, running down to his rowboat.

Pull! Pull! He pulled on the long oars, back down Little Clam Bay toward home.

The little green sailboat was dry when Michael came back to the boat yard after lunch. His mother had cut a sail out of yellow cloth. Michael had a long needle and a long piece of strong thread, too. Both Michael and Mr. Timothy tried to thread the needle. Mr. Timothy tried and tried.

"I can't seem to do it," he said, finally.

Then Mr. Timothy had an idea.

"I know!" he said. "Mrs. Timothy can thread a needle!" Mr. Timothy forgot that he was holding the needle and clapped his hands. "Ouch! Ouch! Michael, go next door and ask Mrs. Timothy to help you."

Michael ran next door to ask Mrs. Timothy to thread his needle. Something that smelled very good was cooking in the house next door. Michael knocked. A smiling little lady in a bright yellow apron came to see who had knocked.

"How do you do, Mrs. Timothy?" said Michael.
"Will you please thread this needle for me?"

"I'll be glad to," said Mrs. Timothy. "Will
you come into the kitchen?"

Michael went into the kitchen with Mrs.
Timothy. There on the table was the biggest
plate of cookies Michael had ever seen.

"Oh, that's what smelled so good," said Michael.

Mrs. Timothy laughed. "Have some," she said.

So Michael did, and the cookies were even
better than they smelled.

"Now, let's see about threading this needle,"
said Mrs. Timothy. She pushed the thread through
the needle's eye so quickly that Michael was
surprised.

"Thank you," he said. "It looks easy when
you do it."

Michael sat on the steps and sewed his yellow sail on to the mast. Round and round the mast, round and round the boom he sewed. At the end, Mrs. Timothy helped him.

"I hope it sails!" Michael said.

"I'm sure it will!" Mrs. Timothy told him.

Michael ran back to the boat yard. Mr. Dan and Mr. Timothy were out on the dock.

"My boat is finished!" called Michael.

"Good! I knew that Mrs. Timothy could thread a needle!" laughed Mr. Timothy. "Let's put the boat into the water as we do a real ship."

"How do we do that?" asked Michael.

"We'll use the dolly," said Mr. Timothy.

"Dolly!" said Michael in surprise. "What do we need a dolly for?"

"This isn't the kind of dolly you think it is," laughed Mr. Dan. "Do you see that track that goes down into the water? That's the runway. Do you see that cart on the runway? That's a dolly," he said.

112

"Oh, now I see," said Michael.

Mr. Dan put the little green boat on the dolly.

"Now we can let the dolly roll down the runway. Watch out! Here it goes!" He untied a rope on a post at the end of the runway. The dolly started rolling toward the water.

"All aboard!" shouted Michael and he jumped on the dolly, too!

"Wait! Stop!" called Mr. Timothy.

But the dolly didn't wait. It rolled faster and faster. Splash! Michael and the dolly dropped into the bay. The wind filled the yellow sail of the little boat and it sailed out past the dock.

Where was Michael? Mr. Timothy and Mr. Dan started to wade in after him. Just then some seaweed rose right out of the water.

"Oh!" came a voice from the seaweed. It was Michael's voice. Michael stood up and waded in to the shore, pulling the seaweed off his head as he came.

Michael saw his little boat sailing away. He ran down the dock and jumped into his own boat. Mr. Timothy pushed Michael's boat away from the dock. Michael pulled on the long oars. Pull! Pull! Pull!

"Give her a race!" Mr. Timothy called.

The little green boat, with its bright yellow sail, was not far ahead of him. He caught up with it just as he reached his own dock.

"It's a fine boat I made in Mr. Timothy's boat yard," thought Michael.

Lois Kimball

THE FISH WITH THE DEEP SEA SMILE

They fished and they fished,
Way down in the sea,
Down in the sea a mile.
They fished among all the fish in the sea
For the fish with the deep sea smile.

One fish came up from the deep of the sea,
From down in the sea a mile.
It had blue-green eyes
And whiskers three,
But never a deep sea smile.

One fish came up from the deep of the sea,
From down in the sea a mile,
With electric lights up and down his tail
But never a deep sea smile.

They fished and they fished,
Way down in the sea,
Down in the sea a mile.

They fished among all the fish in the sea
For the fish with the deep sea smile.

One fish came up with terrible teeth;
One fish with long strong jaws;
One fish came up with long-stalked eyes;
One fish with terrible claws.

They fished all through the ocean deep
For many and many a mile,
And they caught a fish with a laughing eye
But none with a deep sea smile.

And then one day they got a pull
From down in the sea a mile,
And when they pulled the fish into the boat
He smiled a deep sea smile!

And as he smiled, the hook got free
And then, with a deep sea smile,
He flipped his tail and swam away,
Down in the sea a mile.

Margaret Wise Brown

MOVING DAY

Two Wishes

Tommy and Peter lived in the city. Tommy was just eight and Peter was almost seven.

They went to school just around the corner from their own home. But it was summer now, and the boys didn't know what to do with themselves. They couldn't play in the school yard because the gates were all locked. They couldn't play in the street because there were so many automobiles passing all the time. And their own back yard was so very small that the cat next door could cross it in three jumps when she happened to be in a hurry.

"I wish we had a large back yard," said Peter.

"I wish we could do something this summer that we never did before," said Tommy.

They were having supper at the time.

"Two very good wishes," said their father. "I didn't mean to tell you so soon, but on Friday we're moving into a new house. The back yard is larger, and I'm sure that moving is something we don't do very often."

Tommy and Peter stopped eating and looked at Mr. Nelson. He was smiling. Then they looked at their mother. She was smiling, too. Finally they twisted about in their chairs and looked at each other and grinned.

"Hurray!" cried Tommy. "We're going to move."

"You'll have to work hard helping Mother pack," said their father.

"We'll help. Hurray, we're going to move!"

Even little sister began to get excited. "Betty go too," she cried. And she banged her spoon down so hard in her bowl that the milk flew all over her father.

Everybody laughed. Mr. Nelson wiped a drop of milk from his right eye. "You boys go outdoors and play until bedtime," he said. "If you don't, we'll have another one of those wiggle-and-giggle evenings."

Next morning, soon after breakfast, a funny old truck came chug-chugging into the drive and stopped just in front of the garage.

"Is this where Mr. Nelson lives?" asked the driver.

"Yes, sir," Tommy answered. He had to shout to make the man hear him.

The man began to take a great many empty wooden boxes out of the truck. Tommy and Peter hardly saw the boxes at first because they were looking at the funny old truck. It was still chug-chugging away, and it shook so hard that it rattled all over. First came a big shake, then three little shakes, then a big shake again. Every time the big shake came, the boys looked at each other and laughed.

But the man didn't seem to care. He laughed too. "I guess you never saw a truck like that before," he said. He seemed proud that the truck rattled and shook.

When the man had gone, Tommy and Peter were surprised to see how many boxes he had left in their little back yard. Right away they began to pile them on top of each other. They built caves and tunnels, too, and had so much fun that lunch time came before they knew they were hungry.

"As soon as Betty wakes up from her nap," said Mrs. Nelson, "you boys may begin to help me pack."

"What can we pack?" asked Peter.

"First, pack the kitchen things that we won't need right away. Then, if you are very careful, you may pack all our books in the boxes."

Little sister Betty enjoyed the packing just as much as Tommy and Peter. She took books out of one box and put them in another. Sometimes she put them back in the bookcases. She packed her Teddy bear with the knives and forks and spoons.

That evening Mr. Nelson could find only one of his slippers. He looked for the other in every corner of every room in the house. He looked in all the closets and he looked under all the beds. But he couldn't find that other slipper.

"Well," he said at last, "I suppose this is just one of the things that happen when you move into a new house."

He had to go about that evening and the next evening and the next, with one slipper off and one slipper on.

By the end of the third day, the bookcases and the closets and the drawers were all empty. Even the rugs had been cleaned and rolled up against the walls.

"I'm glad we're going to move tomorrow," said Mr. Nelson. He was still hopping about with one slipper off and one slipper on. "We can't find this and we can't find that. I should not be surprised to wake up in the morning and find that we had even packed ourselves."

"What time is the moving van coming?" asked Tommy.

"At one o'clock, right after we've had lunch. That will give us plenty of time to finish our work."

The Moving Van

Friday morning was the longest morning that Tommy and Peter had ever known. They woke up very early and had the wiggles-and-giggles until they had waked up everyone else, too. Mr. Nelson finally came to their bedroom door. His eyes were only half open and his hair stood fiercely on end.

124

"Hurry and get dressed," he said. "That moving van will be here before you know it."

By nine o'clock Tommy and Peter had washed and dressed and eaten their breakfast. They sat on the sofa looking out of the window and waiting for the van. At ten o'clock they went out on the front porch and waited. At eleven they sat on the curb. Still the van did not come.

"Now how long will it be?" asked Tommy for the fourteenth time. He and Peter had been taking turns running into the house to ask that question.

Mr. Nelson looked at Tommy and sighed. He was tired of answering the same question. "I suppose it would be easier if I came out and sat on the curb with you," he said. Then he took off his wrist watch and put it on Tommy's left wrist. "Now you ask yourself what time it is when you want to know. Come in at noon and we'll have that picnic lunch."

The boys loved picnic lunches. But not today.

They came in at noon and drank some milk quickly. Then they took their sandwiches back to the curb with them.

"Now what time is it?" asked Peter.

Tommy looked at the watch on his wrist. "Ten minutes past twelve."

"Is that all?" said Peter. "Probably it has stopped."

Tommy held the watch to his ear and listened. "No, it has not stopped," he said. "But it may be slow."

At last the van appeared round the corner. Tommy and Peter began to jump up and down, shouting, "Here we are! Here we are!"

There were three men on the seat of the big yellow moving van. One of them leaned out.

"Is this where Mr. Spindleshanks lives?" he asked.

Tommy stopped shouting. Mr. Spindleshanks! He could hardly find his voice to say, "No, sir. This is where Mr. Nelson lives."

126

"That's the name," said the man, grinning.
"I knew it was something like Spindleshanks.
Back right up here, Ed."

The first thing that went into the truck was
the piano. The three men put the piano on a
little truck with wheels and loaded it into the
front of the van. After the piano was in, they

began carrying out of the house beds and tables and chairs and rugs and boxes. Tommy and Peter had a hard time trying to follow all three men at the same time. They kept running from one to the other. Finally they ran right into one man who was carrying a big chair over his head and couldn't very well see where he was going. He almost fell down.

At last the men went into the house to make sure that nothing had been left behind. Tommy and Peter were right at their heels. Then, before they knew what was happening, one of the men picked them both up by the back of their overalls and carried them into the living room.

"Here's something I almost forgot," he said. "Where shall I pack these two pieces of furniture?"

Mr. Nelson laughed when he saw Tommy and Peter kicking their feet in the air.

"I'll take them in my car," he said. "One of them has on my wrist watch, and I won't be able to tell the time without him."

128

At first the boys and their little sister rode backwards in the car, with their knees on the seat and their noses against the back window.

"Please go faster," said Tommy. "The van is right behind us."

Mr. Nelson tried to see the van, but there were too many heads in the way. "Suppose you all turn around and watch where we're going," he said. "We're almost in the country now."

"Why," said Tommy. "We must be going to move to a different city."

"How long before we get to our new house?" asked Peter.

"At least two hours," said Mr. Nelson. "We can't run away and leave the van. It won't know where to go."

"Let's have a game," said Tommy. "You take your side of the road, Peter, and I'll take my side. Then we'll try to guess which is our new house."

"I guess that place," said Peter, when they had gone another mile.

Mr. Nelson shook his head.

"I guess that one," said Tommy.

Again Mr. Nelson shook his head.

Whenever they passed through a town or village, Peter guessed every house on the left side of the road and Tommy guessed every house on the right side.

"We'll have to give up that game," said Mr. Nelson at last. "If I shake my head once more, I'm afraid it will fall off."

A long time later, when it was growing dark and there wasn't a town in sight, Mr. Nelson turned the car into a country road. He stopped it beside the very largest house the boys had ever seen.

"Well," he said, "here we are at last."

Tommy and Peter followed him into the house. They were too surprised to say anything. They had never dreamed that their new home was to be in the country. It was the best surprise they had ever had. They began running up and down the stairs and from one room to another as fast as they could go.

"There are five rooms downstairs and six rooms upstairs," cried Tommy, all out of breath.

"I know it," said Peter. "I guess this is the biggest farmhouse in the whole world. Let's go out and see our back yard before it gets too dark."

They ran downstairs again and reached the door just in time to run into the moving man who was carrying that same chair over his head again. For a second time, he almost fell down.

"Well, well!" he said. "This chair certainly brings me bad luck."

When the boys came back into the house again, the van was gone. Mr. Nelson had set up the stove in the kitchen and Mrs. Nelson was getting supper. Supper smelled good. But Tommy and Peter looked about them sadly, not saying a word.

Mr. Nelson stared at them in surprise. "Why the long faces?" he asked. "Don't you like our new home?"

"It has no back yard," said Peter sadly.

Mr. Nelson laughed. "You mean it has no fence around it, Peter. This is a farm and it is all back yard. It has a brook and a pond and apple trees and pastures and everything. You just wait until morning."

Tommy and Peter looked at each other. Then, for the second time that day, they had the wiggles-and-giggles. But they were so hungry and so tired and so sleepy that this time the wiggles-and-giggles didn't last very long.

Earl M. Rush

THE LITTLE OLD COUNTRY CAR

An Important Question

Once upon a time there was a Little Old Country Car. One bumper was broken. One spring was broken. One door rattled. But the Little Old Country Car got about the country just the same!

One day Father said, "Let's turn in this old car. What does he do to earn his gas and oil?"

"Oh, dear me!" cried the Little Old Country Car, who did not wish to be turned in. "What do I do? What do other cars do? What does anybody do?"

So he started out into the great wide world to find out what cars did to earn their gas and oil. He backed quietly out of the garage and ran down the road.

Down the dirt road he went until he came to
a highway. Down the highway he went as fast
as he could go. Cars ran this way. Cars ran that
way. Big cars, little cars, trucks, and busses.

"My goodness!" cried the Little Old Country
Car. "I never knew there were so many cars
in the world. What do all these cars do to earn
their gas and oil?"

Suddenly the Little Old Country Car heard a
"Honk! Honk! Honk!" behind him. He gave
such a jump that he almost stalled his engine.
He could feel a hot breath on his tail light. He
looked back and saw a great green moving van.
134

The Little Old Country Car asked, "What do you do to earn your gas and oil? Bump other cars?"

"What do I do to earn my gas and oil?" honked the moving van. "I move people from house to house. I move their chairs and tables, beds and babies. I have a hard life."

"You certainly do," said the Little Old Country Car. "Why do people want to move their chairs and tables, beds and babies?"

"Don't ask me!" honked the van. "Don't ask them. They don't know why. I don't know why. Sometimes I work all day. Sometimes I work all night. Everybody always wants to move at the same time."

There was no more time for questions. The big green moving van passed the little car. "Good luck," he called.

"Well, I can't move people with their tables and chairs, their beds and babies," sighed the Little Old Country Car. "I'm not big enough."

135

Down the highway ran the Little Old Country Car. Cars ran this way. Cars ran that way. He had never seen so many cars before. He ran on and on until he came to the great city.

The Little Old Country Car turned to his left over a long bridge.

"Clang! Clang! Clang!" sounded a fierce bell. The Little Old Country Car put on his brakes just in time. A great red car swung around the corner. It pulled up beside the curb and came to a sudden stop. Men jumped off and began running this way and that.

"My goodness!" cried the Little Old Country Car. "Who are you and what do you do to earn your gas and oil?"

"I'm a fire engine!" roared the red car.

"Do you set things on fire?" asked the Little Old Country Car.

"I do not!" roared the fire engine. He grew

136

redder at the very idea. "I put out fires!"

"Oh, I see," said the Little Old Country Car.
"I'm sorry."

He had no more time for questions. A policeman
shouted to him to move on. The Little Old
Country Car turned down a side street. As he
went along, he came to a deep hole beside the
road.

The Little Old Country Car went as close as
he dared to the hole. At the bottom he saw
something as big as an elephant. It had no wheels,

but it looked like a car just the same. With its two huge jaws it was biting out dirt and rock from a bank. Then it dumped the rock and dirt into a truck.

"What do you do to earn your gas and oil?" asked the Little Old Country Car.

But all the queer big thing would answer was:

"Bite and dig all day!

No rest! No play!"

Then it bit out more dirt and rock and dumped it with a rattle and bang into a waiting truck.

"Dear, dear," thought the Little Old Country Car. "I can't do that to earn my gas and oil." So he ran on down the street.

Suddenly he heard a rumbling beside him, and there was a strange-looking truck. Its body kept turning round and round and round. Water and mud came out of it.

"Who are you?" cried the Little Old Country Car in surprise.

"I'm a cement mixer," came a deep voice from way down in the truck.

"What do you do to earn your gas and oil?" asked the little car. "Get mixed up?"

"I never get mixed up," answered the cement mixer. "I mix everything else up. That's what I do."

On down the street it went, turning round and round and round as it went.

"Queer," thought the Little Old Country Car. "I should not like to earn my gas and oil that way." He had no more time for thought.

139

"L-o-o-k o-u-t!" came a long loud whistle.

The little car hurried to one side. A fierce-looking little truck, painted bright red, went past him. It had EXPLOSIVES in big letters on it.

"What do you do to earn your gas and oil?" asked the Little Old Country Car. "Blow things up?"

"Not unless things run into me!" answered the bright red truck.

The Little Old Country Car waited quietly until the red truck was out of sight. Then he started on. He was growing tired of the city. He wanted to be at home again in the country.

As the day went on, the Little Old Country Car grew very tired. More and more he wanted to be back in the country again.

"I don't like city life," thought the Little Old Country Car. "I could never earn my gas and oil here."

Just then the little car stopped.

Around the corner came a wrecking car, pulling another car behind it.

"My goodness!" cried the Little Old Country Car. "What did you do to that car? Did you wreck it?"

"No such thing!" answered the wrecking car. "Cars wreck themselves. I have to pick them up and take them home. Some run into trees. Some run into each other. They keep me busy. You have no idea how many silly cars there are on the road."

"Dear, dear," said the Little Old Country Car.

"You may be sending for me yourself some day," called the wrecking car.

"I certainly hope not!" thought the Little Old Country Car.

"I'm going home even if they turn me in," he sighed. But which way should he go to get to the country?

The Little Old Country Car saw a mail truck standing at the curb. He stopped beside the mail truck and said politely, "Can you tell me the way to the country?"

"What country?" asked the mail truck. "Canada? Mexico?"

"Oh, I don't mean that kind of country," explained the little car. "I mean the kind of country where you see grass and trees and cows."

"I never saw a letter to a grass, or a tree, or a cow," sniffed the mail truck. "There's a police car over there. Ask him."

Across the street stood a small police car with two large policemen in it.

142

"What has happened to you?" asked the Little Old Country Car. "Did you get a ticket?"

"Certainly not!" said the car. "I give tickets. I'm a police car."

"Can you tell me the way to the country?" asked the Little Old Country Car.

"Straight ahead over the bridge and turn right. Then follow Route 100," said the police car.

Just then there came a call from the police station, "Calling all cars. Calling all cars." Down the street ran the police car.

"So that's what he does to earn his gas and oil," sighed the Little Old Country Car sadly. "Now for Route 100."

"R-o-u-t-e 100," came a low purr behind him. He looked back and saw a great bus.

"Is this the right way to the country?" asked the Little Old Country Car.

"Follow me and I'll take you all the way across the country and back again," said the bus.

"I only want to get home, back to the country," said the little car. "I ran away because I was afraid they were going to turn me in. But now I think I will go home anyway."

"Very well," said the bus. "Stay at home and be turned in if you wish." The bus ran on ahead and the Little Old Country Car watched until it went around a bend in the road. But the Little Old Country Car did not care, for at the next corner he saw a sign, ROUTE 100.

On and on went the Little Old Country Car. At last he left the city behind. At last he saw green grass and trees along the road. The Little Old Country Car was so happy that he began to run more slowly.

Suddenly he ran around a bend in the road and saw a queer, long, low truck. It was three times as long as any truck he had seen before. On its back it was carrying six shiny new cars, all painted different colors.

"Where are you going?" asked the Little Old Country Car.

"We're new cars on the way to the city," called the six new cars. "What good times we shall have!" And down the road they went.

The Little Old Country Car stopped to watch them go. Then he sighed. Once he had been new, too, but now he was old and going to be turned in. He was going to be turned in because he did not earn his gas and oil. The Little Old Country Car sighed again and ran on his way.

Just then he saw another truck coming down the road. It was an open truck, and it was carrying a horse. The horse's head stuck out over the back of the truck.

"Well!" cried the Little Old Country Car. "Having a ride? You don't know how silly you look!"

"You don't know how silly I feel!" snapped the horse, as he passed. "You should not make fun of me. I hope you have a blowout!"

And sure enough, just then one tire went bang! The Little Old Country Car had to stop at the next garage to have it changed. It was late in the afternoon when he climbed up the last hill that led toward home.

As he reached his own gate, he saw a terrible sight. His engine almost stalled. He could not even blow his horn. A beautiful new car stood in front of the garage. He was too late.

Then Mother saw him. "Here's the little old car," she cried to Father. "What are you going to do with him?"

"I was going to turn him in," said Father.

"Oh, no!" said Mother. "You have the new car. The children and I would like to use the old one."

"Yes, yes," cried the children, and they all jumped up and down.

The Little Old Country Car gave a great sigh of happiness. He was not to be turned in! With a honk he ran into the garage and stopped his engine.

"I'm so glad that we have a two-car garage," said Mother.

The next day, the Little Old Country Car started in to earn his gas and oil.

He took the children to school.

He did the marketing.

He took Mother to a meeting.

He picked up hot rolls for lunch.

He met the children at the ball field.

He took them all to the moving pictures.

"How could we ever get along without the little old car?" said Mother, as the days and the weeks and the months went by. "I'm glad we didn't turn him in. He certainly earns his gas and oil!"

Caroline D. Emerson

149

STUNT SATURDAY

BAD NEWS

Jacob Pulaski hurried away from school by himself, feeling very unhappy. That afternoon Miss Adams had told Jacob's class about the Stunt Night that was to be held at their school the next Saturday. Boys and girls from other schools were

150

to come and take part. The prize for the best stunt was to be a trip to Washington, D. C. Every boy and girl in Jacob's class wanted to win that prize.

Just as Jacob started down the hill toward home, Milt Jones and Jack Avery rode by on bicycles. They waved and Jacob waved back, but seeing them made him feel still more unhappy. Those boys could do stunts! Milt played the harmonica and Jack did card tricks. It seemed to Jacob that every American boy and girl could do some sort of stunt. Only he himself, Jacob Pulaski, who was born in Poland, did not know how to do a single stunt.

Soon Jacob came to his father's farm. He saw the neat buildings on the hillside. He looked at the fat cows coming home to be milked. All this farm belonged to the Pulaskis because the whole family had worked together for it and had worked hard. Jacob knew that was something to be proud of, for they had been in America only five years. Just now Jacob wished that his family had spent less time working and more time doing stunts.

On most days he went right into the house to see Mother. Today he spent a long time outside, feeding the pigs and the chickens. He knew Mother would guess that something was wrong as soon as she saw him. It made her feel sad when Jacob thought that he was different from other boys in school. And today he felt very different.

It was nearly time for supper when Jacob at last went up to the house. All the rest of the family were inside. Jacob heard Uncle John's fiddle, and then he saw that his little sister Anna was dancing. Her short legs flew. Her full skirts fluttered. She was trying to dance the mazurka that he had taught her.

Jacob hurried in. He pulled off his cap and coat and danced out onto the kitchen floor with Anna.

152

"Hi, Jacob! Ho, Anna!" Uncle John shouted over his fiddle. Father and Mother beat time. The two children danced until they were out of breath. When the dance was over, they sank down on the floor like tired puppies.

Mother set out the cabbage soup in the blue bowls on the table. "You've done well," she told Jacob. "It is—how do you say it in America?— it is a stunt to teach so little a girl the mazurka."

Jacob took his spoon out of the good soup and stared at his mother. She had given him an idea. If it was a stunt to teach the mazurka, then perhaps it would be a stunt to dance it next Saturday!

The next minute he knew that wouldn't do after all. He could not dance the mazurka by himself. He needed Uncle John to play the fiddle. He needed Mother and Father to beat time. He needed little Anna to dance with him.

Jacob sighed. Uncle John and Mother both looked at him.

"What's the trouble?" Uncle John said.

For a minute Jacob didn't say anything. Then he told them. "It's Stunt Night at our school next Saturday. Everyone in my class can do a stunt except me. I—I was thinking I might do a mazurka."

154

"But why can't you?" Mrs. Pulaski asked.

"Because—because I can't do it alone."

Uncle John laughed his big, cheerful laugh. "Don't let that trouble you," he said. "We'll all help. I play the fiddle. Anna dances. Mama and Papa beat time."

"I'm afraid that wouldn't do," Jacob began.

"Oh, come now," Uncle John said. "You mustn't be afraid. Think of our brave Polish General Kosciusko. Think of General Pulaski, whose name we have. He gave his life to help win the American Revolution. They were not afraid."

"We will make a new dress for Anna," Mrs. Pulaski put in, "a real Polish dress for the Polish mazurka."

Jacob bit his lips and said nothing. It was not that he was afraid. The other boys and girls in his class could do stunts by themselves. He knew very well that they did not need to have their whole family help them.

Stunt Saturday came all too quickly for Jacob. It seemed to him that it was no time at all before the whole Pulaski family piled into the old farm truck to go to the school.

On the way over, the Jones family passed them in their car. Milt leaned out of the window and called, "Hi, Jacob, how would you like that trip to Washington?"

Jacob couldn't even grin back. He had hardly given a thought to the trip. He had thought only about how he could get through the stunt. Right now he wished with all his heart that the truck would break down so that none of them could get to the school.

Just then Anna put her warm little hand in his. "I won't be afraid," she said, "not when I dance with you."

Jacob looked down at her and he knew that it did not matter what his class thought. He must

156

do the best he could for the sake of his family. They had all tried so hard to help him.

"Hello, Jacob," Miss Adams said when they reached the school. "We are nearly ready to begin. Your stunt will be number four. What shall I call it?"

"A—a Polish dance," Jacob said, wishing that he could drop out of sight. "A—a mazurka. My family—that is, my little sister—wants to be in it, too."

Miss Adams nodded her head. "Why, yes," she said. "We'll be glad to have her."

The stunts began. Milt played on his harmonica.
A little girl from another school did a fancy dance.
Jack Avery did his card tricks. Jacob came next.

He took Anna's hand and they went up to the
stage with Uncle John right behind them. Uncle
John stood at one side of the stage and began to
play the first gay notes of the mazurka. Jacob
threw back his head. He saw Mother and Father
sitting close together in the front row. Their hands
were out, waiting to beat time.

Anna's hand felt cold in Jacob's. He held it
tighter and smiled down at her. Suddenly Uncle
John called out, "Ready? Mazurka!"

158

Anna smiled bravely back at Jacob, and they began to dance. They kicked and spun and whirled through the steps they knew so well. "Hi! Mazurka!" called Uncle John at the end of the first dance.

"Hi!" shouted Father. "Hi! Hi!" called Mother, and they all beat time.

Jacob hardly stopped for breath before he and Anna were off again. At the very end Jacob lifted little Anna right off her feet and whirled her around the stage.

"Hurrah! Hurrah!" Shouts and cheers came from all over the room. Jacob and Anna bowed. Then, while people still cheered, they went back and sat with the family.

Jacob watched the rest of the stunts with his head in a whirl. He could not believe it! People had liked the mazurka! They had liked little Anna, and Uncle John, and they had liked Mother and Father beating time.

In what seemed a very short time the show was over. Soon Miss Adams went up on the stage. "I am sure we all agree with the judges," she said. "The prize goes to Jacob Pulaski. I am only sorry that we can't send all of his family to Washington."

Jacob's heart beat very hard as he, too, went up on the stage. Miss Adams and the judges had liked the dance; better still, they had liked his family. They had liked everything so much that they were sending him to Washington!

Miss Adams shook Jacob's hand. "The prize is a good American trip," she said, "for a fine American boy."

Lavinia Davis

161

TORNADO WEATHER

RUN FOR THE CELLAR

What a hot day! Helen dropped down on the front porch swing and shut her eyes. She couldn't remember another day so hot as this one. Even her puppy just lay there with his little black sides panting.

Dad had driven to town in the truck to get Pete, the hired man. Lee and Bill, Helen's brothers, were working on an old bicycle out by the back porch. Helen wished she had gone with Dad. Even the hot ride into town would have been better than this.

She shut her eyes again. How hot it was! How quiet! Far down the road she could hear a truck rattling along. Then the truck came around the corner and up the drive. As it stopped, Dad and Pete jumped out and ran for the porch.

162

"Helen, a tornado's coming," Dad called. "We're right in its way. Run for the cellar! Don't stop, Helen. Run for the cellar!"

Dad had often told them that this might happen. They must all get into the tornado cellar before the black whirling funnel of wind reached their farm.

Quickly Helen picked up her puppy and raced around back to the tornado cellar. It had a door that opened right into the side of a little grassy hill. They kept vegetables in it in winter, since tornadoes come only in the summer.

Helen pushed and pushed, but the wooden door would not open. High above her, the yellow sky was just as still as before. Far out over the cornfields she saw the great black funnel of wind, its long tail reaching down. Helen could hear the wind roar far away. She knew that no one had ever been able to tell how fast tornadoes whirl. She pushed her shoulder against the door until it opened a little.

Lee and Bill came running up behind her, looking very frightened. Bill was dragging his dog, Shep, by the collar. The boys pushed against the cellar door, too, and it slowly came open. It was dark inside. A smell of earth and vegetables came to them as they fell in.

Helen turned to look back and saw her mother running from the house. As she, too, came into the dark cellar, she fell over Shep. He barked and jumped back.

Then Dad and Pete bent down to get in through the low door. Dad took a last look at the yellow sky and fastened the door behind him.

Everything was dark.

"Is everybody here?" Dad shouted, although they could all hear him easily.

"Yes, Will," Mother's voice answered. "But I left some of the windows open upstairs."

"Well, you can't go back now. We're just in time as it is. But we're all safe. A tornado does not harm anything under the ground."

Through the thick earth walls they could hear the roar of the wind growing louder and louder. Helen lay flat on the damp ground, afraid that the tornado might take the grass roof off their cellar. The roar was very loud and the ground shook. There was a loud crash and then another.

"What was that?" Mother asked.

Dad's voice sounded queer when he answered. "I don't know. One of the buildings, perhaps."

Suddenly everything was quiet outside. No one

166

said a word. It was so quiet that Helen wondered if the end of the world had come. Then they heard little pattering sounds.

"The rain," Dad and Mother said together.

"That means it's all over," Dad called out. "You and the children stay here while I go and see what has happened."

WIND AND MUD

Helen and Bill and Lee couldn't wait. They came out of the cellar with Mother and Dad. Rain beat on their faces, but the light seemed so bright that they stood there, all of them, and blinked for a minute. Even when their eyes grew used to the light, Helen still blinked because she couldn't believe what she saw.

She was looking right at the place where the house should have been. It was not there. She saw the stone cellar steps and the front steps but the rest of the house was gone.

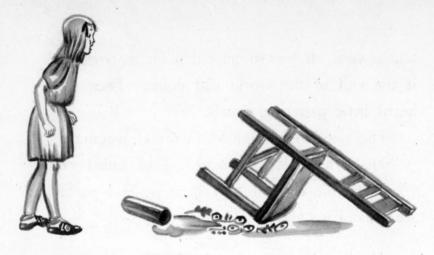

"Look," Bill shouted, and pointed out beyond the barn. In the middle of the field, one hundred feet away, sat their house, as if it belonged there.

The rain was still beating down, and Helen's wet hair was hanging around her shoulders as she raced over to the house. The windows were all broken and the door of the front porch was hanging open. Helen had to pull herself up into the front door because the steps were gone.

It was their house all right, but what a sight it was inside! The chairs and tables had been knocked over. Everything near the windows was dirty. The dust from the whirling cloud was

thick on the floor. Wherever the rain came
pouring in through the broken windows, it turned
the dust to mud.

Helen jumped down from the front door and
ran around the barn to find the boys.

"Bill," she called, "Did you see the inside—"
But her mouth just stayed open without finishing
what she was going to say.

There stood the boys and her father in the
spot where the windmill had been half an hour
before. All around them were little pieces of

169

wood and iron. Even the thick iron rods of the windmill were lying on the ground, twisted as though they were made of straw.

The rain had stopped and Mother came running across the field. Her shoes were covered with mud.

"Will," she called, "I have looked at the kitchen, and if you can believe it, the things are almost all in place. As soon as I clean off the dust, I'll get supper."

"Fine!" Dad said. "We've been pretty lucky. The tornado moved the house only a little way and we can put it back all right. It might have been broken up like this windmill. The barn and the animals were not touched at all." Then he turned to Lee and Bill. "Boys," he said, "you run and get water from the well for your mother to clean with, or we'll have nothing but mud soup for supper."

Marguerite Hurrey

REALLY TRUE

THE FIRST BALLOON RIDE

Get up, Louis, get up. Have you forgotten what day this is?"

Louis rolled over in bed and pushed his long dark hair out of his eyes. He was very sleepy.

"What day is it, Mother?" he asked.

But before she had time to tell him, he remembered.

"The balloon!" he cried. "This is the day I'm going to see the big balloon go up in the palace garden."

His mother brought out his Sunday suit, and his best shoes. He climbed down from his high bed and began to dress himself.

"Do you think it will go clear to the sky, Mother? Will it go as high as the clouds?"

"They say it will go very, very high," she answered. "Hold still while I tie back your hair."

Louis looked down at his best shoes.

"I hope the King sees me," he said.

"The King of France won't be looking for the son of his gardener," said his mother. "Stay beside the bushes and be quiet, as your father told you."

Louis nodded. "I will try to be quiet. But let me go now, Mother. It's such a long walk, and I

do want to be there on time. I can eat my breakfast on the way."

His mother laughed. "You won't be late," she answered. She gave him a roll and a pickle, and he started out.

When he came to the palace garden, Louis saw the balloon. It was made of strong paper, stretched over a wooden frame, and was painted in bright colors.

"It doesn't look as if it would ever go up in the sky," thought Louis. "I wonder what makes it fly."

He saw a man standing near by and asked, "What makes it fly?"

The man smiled. "We make a fire under it," he said. "That fills the balloon with smoke and hot air. You will see in a little while."

Just then another man drove up in a cart.

"Here we are, Joseph," he called. "Here are our passengers."

"Passengers?" said Louis. "Is someone going up in the balloon?"

"Not in the balloon," the man answered. "The passengers will ride in a basket that is tied under the balloon."

"They must be very brave," said Louis.

The two men laughed. "Oh, they are brave," said Joseph. "Come here and take a look at them."

Louis climbed up on the wheel of the cart and looked into it. There stood a sheep, a duck, and a rooster.

"You see," Joseph went on, "we couldn't find a man who was brave enough. No one knows what the air is like so high above the earth. A man might not be able to live up there. So we are sending up these passengers first. If they come down safely, a man may go next time."

176

Louis nodded. "You seem to know all about it," he said.

The man laughed again. "We should know about it," answered Joseph. "My brother and I made this balloon."

"You did!" cried Louis in surprise. "Did you really!"

The brothers put the sheep, the duck, and the rooster into the basket. Then they waited for the King to come out of his palace. It seemed to Louis that he would never come. At last the King took his place, and the Queen sat beside him. On the other side of the garden a great crowd was watching.

Next, Joseph made a fire of damp straw. The smoke and hot air filled the balloon just as he had said it would. The balloon pulled at the ropes that held it to the ground.

"Let it go," cried Joseph.

The men cut the ropes. As the balloon rose in the air, carrying its three passengers, everyone cheered. Louis wondered how the sheep and the duck and the rooster felt, sailing up there above the trees.

Louis ran along the ground, hoping he would be near enough to see the balloon come down. Joseph and his brother ran, too.

"It's landing," called Joseph. "It's landing! How long has it been in the air?"

"Eight minutes," said his brother. "I wonder how the animals are."

He soon found out. The sheep was chewing as quietly as if it had never left the ground. The duck was all right, too. Joseph picked up the rooster.

"Something is the matter with him," he said.

His brother looked at the rooster carefully.

"He has a broken wing," he said. "Perhaps the sheep kicked him."

They looked at the sheep, but he went right on chewing.

"Just like a sheep," said Louis.

178

"Don't you make fun of that sheep," laughed Joseph. "He has helped show that we need not be afraid to fly."

He turned to the other people who had followed them from the palace gardens.

"The animals are all right," he shouted. "It's safe to go up in the air."

Once again the people cheered and Louis shouted, "Hurray!"

Robin Palmer

CRAZY RIDER

Father and Mother sat in the front seat of the automobile. Jane and Billy sat in the back. Father was driving, and Mother was looking at a road map.

"Soon," said Mother, "we shall come to the Bad Lands." In five minutes they were there.

At Cedar Pass they got out of the car and stood for a long time looking out over the Bad Lands. As far as they could see were steep and pointed hills. These hills had stripes of red, and yellow, and white, with purple shadows. No green grass was on the ground between the hills, and the few small cedar trees looked black.

After a while, they went into a shop, where they saw beautiful Indian blankets and Indian pottery. It was so warm that they went into the lunch room, and each had some ice cream. Then Mother and Father went back to look at the blankets and pottery, and Jane and Billy went outside. Around the corner of the building they found an Indian tepee. Three Indians were sitting on the ground just outside the tepee door.

One was a man who wore a bright red shirt. One was a very fat woman in a purple dress. And one was an old, old woman, with a blanket around her. Only her wrinkled face and her white hair were showing.

Billy asked if he might take a picture of them. They smiled and nodded, so he took a picture of all three of them together. Then he took another of the old woman, who had fallen asleep.

"What is her name?" Jane asked the man.

The man turned and spoke to her.

She opened her eyes and nodded, grinning.

"She will tell you a story about her name," said the man to Jane and Billy. "She does not speak English, so I will tell you what she says."

Jane and Billy sat down, and the old woman began to speak. This is the story she told.

When I was a girl, I wanted my own way. I did many foolish things.

Once our village of thirty tepees made camp one day's ride from the Black Hills. We were on a big hunting trip, and the country was strange to many of us.

I was nine snows old.

This is the way it happened.

Everything that my brother Tall Bird did, I did, too. I could run, and swim, and ride a horse just as well as he could.

Everywhere that Tall Bird went, I wanted to go.

But the time came when Tall Bird must go for the first time to hunt buffaloes.

The young men said to me, laughing, "Girls do not hunt buffaloes!" And, laughing, they all rode out of camp. Tall Bird went with them, leaving me behind.

183

I was angry. I was very angry. The anger
went into my heart and made it bad. Then I
saw a fine spotted horse tied behind a tepee.
Quickly I untied him and jumped on his back.
I rode quickly out of the village. I went alone
into the bare brown hills, but the young men
were gone. I could not see them anywhere, and
my heart was bad with anger.

I rode for a long, long time. The brown hills
were gone. They had turned into red, and yellow,
and white hills. They were pointed and steep.

There was no grass growing on them. The sun
was very hot. It was bad country, but my eyes
did not really see it, because my heart was full
of anger. I rode on and on.

Then, suddenly, the anger went out of my
heart and my eyes. Between the steep red hills
there was a great cloud of yellow dust, and under
it were running many, many buffaloes. They
were coming straight toward me!

The high hills were close on both sides of them.
I tried to turn the horse to run away. But that
fine spotted horse was a buffalo-hunting horse!

185

He thought I was a hunter and wanted to kill the buffaloes. He began to gallop straight toward them. I pulled his head around with the rope, and still he galloped toward the buffaloes.

Suddenly the dust and the buffaloes were all around me. One big buffalo struck my horse! I flew up in the air. I turned round and round. I came down. I came down on the back of the buffalo!

It was a long time, a very long time, that I rode on the back of that buffalo. My eyes were full of dust. My heart grew small, and my tongue grew thick with dust. When at last the young men came along on their horses, I could not speak. But I could hear! I could hear them laughing. They laughed a long time.

Because I could not speak, they said, "The buffalo has taken away her tongue! Look! She is yellow with dust like the buffalo. She has turned into a buffalo. The man who marries her will have a buffalo-cow for a wife!"

186

That night the whole village was laughing. Even my brother Tall Bird laughed. My heart was on the ground with sadness. Never again did I want to go out hunting with the young men.

Many, many moons passed before they forgot to laugh about my ride on the buffalo. They named me "Crazy Rider."

Why?

Because I was riding that buffalo backwards!

The old woman laughed, and the other Indians laughed, too. Jane and Billy laughed with them.

By this time it was nearly sunset, and the red light of the sun made the hills of the Bad Lands look even redder than before.

Jane and Billy and Mother and Father stood watching the sunset. When the sun had gone, the hills were blue and purple and the air was cool. The stars came out.

"It is very beautiful here," said Mother. "I think it would be nice to stay here tonight, instead of going on."

"That is a good idea," said Father. "Then we shall have time to watch the Indian dances this evening."

Jane and Billy thought this was a fine idea.

"Maybe Crazy Rider will tell us another story!" they said.

But Father was thinking about something else now. "I'm hungry," said he. "Let's eat!"

Jane Bateman

LITTLE BLACKNOSE

All Aboard!

Excursion! Excur-sh-sh-ion! Excur-sh-sh-sh-ion! Excur-sh-sh-sh-ion!"

Little Blacknose stood puffing and coughing at the Albany end of his track. It was a hot day in August over a hundred years ago.

The sun was pouring down and Little Blacknose was terribly hot. Great crowds of people were rushing and pushing and laughing around him. They were all looking at him. They were all talking about him. They all wanted to ride on him. It was terrible!

"What am I to do?" thought Blacknose. "Where will they go? Will they ride me like a horse?"

He kept on puffing and coughing.

189

"Make way for the Ex-Governor! Make way for the Ex-Governor!"

The crowd moved back to make way for two men who came toward Blacknose. He saw a jolly fat man with a round front like his own boiler. One man held a bottle, and the other man carried a large wreath of flowers. He gave the wreath to the engineer, who fastened it on the front of Little Blacknose. Then the other man climbed up and broke the bottle over his back.

"I name you for the best governor New York State ever had! I name you DeWitt Clinton!" the big man roared.

The crowd roared back. It roared louder and louder, but this time Little Blacknose didn't mind. He liked it.

"They have given me a name, another name! Now I am not just an iron horse. I am Blacknose and I am DeWitt Clinton. I'll show them, I'll show them! Excursion! Excur-sh-sh-sh-ion! Excur-sh-sh-sh-sh-sh-ion!"

Blacknose saw a little boy holding the hand of a nice-looking man with a tall hat on his head and a big brown cigar in his mouth. Blacknose looked at the hat. Blacknose looked at the cigar.

"The man's smoke doesn't come out of his smokestack," he thought. "I wonder why."

The little boy and his father rushed right up to a man who was holding some tickets in his hand.

"Have you our tickets?" the man asked. "We ordered them in Albany."

"Are you Mr. Beers, and is this child Thomas Beers? Yes, sir? Then these are your tickets, for sure."

The man gave one ticket to the little boy and one to his father and walked away.

"Tickets! Tickets!" puffed Little Blacknose. "Whatever in the world are tickets for? And where can these people ride? Choo! Choo! Choo! Not on my boiler! I do not choose to take them! Choo! Choo! Choo! I do not choo-choo-choose!"

Then, as if in answer, there came a terrible bang. Something ran into the poor little engine from behind so hard that he jumped. He looked back along his boiler and found that a wooden platform on four wheels was being fastened onto him. Two big barrels filled with wood stood on the platform-car.

"Well, I shall have plenty of wood to eat on this excursion," thought Blacknose.

Then came another bang. This time something very big and bright and yellow was being fastened by a chain to the platform-car. This new thing that was being fastened on was really the first passenger car. Only it wasn't in the least like a car. It was just a big wooden stagecoach on four wheels, with a round body. Little steps led up into it. There were two long seats, where people could sit facing each other. There were two long seats on top, too, and these were perhaps the nicest seats of all. Inside and outside, there was room for just seventeen people.

193

Little Tommy Beers called to his father, "Oh, Father, please let's sit on top. Let's sit on top! Oh, Father, we must sit on top!" And his father said, "Yes." So up went little Tommy Beers, over the wheel and on top. He was the first passenger to climb aboard the DeWitt Clinton.

Pretty soon another coach was fastened to the first one, and then another and another and another. Little Blacknose stood at the end of a long line of cars. He was puffing and coughing, and wondering how he could ever pull them all!

194

"Ugh! Ugh! Ugh!" he coughed. "I'm afraid I can't do this. I really am afraid I can't do this."

You see, Blacknose had never had to pull or carry anything or anyone but the engineer and himself. Suddenly he saw an ugly old horse, standing right in front of the crowd, laughing at him. There were lots of other horses near by, too. They all turned to listen when the ugly old horse began to laugh.

"Ho, ho, ho!" laughed the horse. "You'll never pull that load. No, not you! It takes five horses to pull five coaches. Can one iron horse do the work of five? No, not you!"

"All aboard!" cried the conductor. He climbed up on a little seat at the back of the platform-car and blew on a tin horn. The coaches were crowded with people, laughing and cheering.

"All aboard! All aboard! Toot! Toot! Toot!"

THREE SURPRISES

The engineer fed a fresh lot of wood into the fire-box. Little Blacknose shook and shook. He pulled and pulled.

"Choo! Choo! Choo!" he coughed. "I'll go if I choo—choo—choose! Choo! Choo!"

Now he was near the ugly old horse who had laughed at him.

"Choo!" he coughed louder than ever.

The horse turned on his heels, and ran and ran and ran—and all the other horses turned on their heels and ran, too. Carts were turned over, vegetables fell out, and ladies were thrown out on their heads in the dirt.

"Ha, ha, ha, ha, ha! Go to grass, you silly old horses!" laughed Little Blacknose.

He laughed and laughed and laughed, as he pulled his five cars faster and faster and faster along the shining rails.

Soon Little Blacknose had gone so fast and so far that he was getting terribly thirsty. The engineer knew that his engine needed water. He put on the brake and slowed down, so that Little Blacknose could stop for a long drink at a watering station beside the track. But when Blacknose tried to stop, something hit him terribly hard from behind. Crash! Crash!

He heard a man shout, "Tommy!" He felt the engineer jump down from behind. He knew that something terrible had happened.

What had he done? Was the little boy hurt— the nice little boy that wanted to sit on top?

Little Blacknose tried to look back along his boiler, but he couldn't see anything. What should he do? Oh, what should he do?

Then the engineer and the conductor jumped back on him once more. The engineer gave him a nice long drink of cool water. He heard the engineer laughing.

"It was just like a child, not to hang on tight. It did not hurt him," the engineer said.

And the conductor laughed as he answered, "Those poor ladies, they did look frightened. We never thought that when we stopped quickly those coaches would bang together. Now we've put the pieces of wood between them, all will be well."

Yes, all was well. So Little Blacknose started on again.

"On again! On again! On again! Schenectady, Schenectady, Schenectady!" he sang happily to himself. And then he tried, "I like Excursions, I like Excursions, I like Excursions!" and found it a good song.

He had come almost to Schenectady when he heard voices calling, "Fire! Fire! Help! Fire!"

Again Blacknose stopped quickly. Looking back along his boiler, he saw a lady on the top of the first coach jumping up and down, while a man seemed to be trying to put her head in a coat! It seemed very queer. Soon they held up a round red thing, and then he couldn't see any more. But the engineer was laughing again when he came back to start once more.

"We must find a way to make you eat your sparks, little iron horse," he laughed. "You can't go setting fire to ladies' hats any more!"

"Schenectady, Schenectady, Schenectady!" At last Little Blacknose pulled his long train of shining yellow coaches up beside the Schenectady station and stood puffing in the middle of a great crowd of people.

"Isn't he a wonder!" they cried.

"Isn't he a wonder!" yelled Tommy Beers.

"Isn't he a wonder!" cried the lady whose hat he had set on fire. They all cheered him. They all cried, "Hurray for Blacknose! Hurray for the DeWitt Clinton! Hurray for the first excursion!"

And then all the people he had carried went into Schenectady to eat a big dinner. Little Blacknose settled down to enjoy a rest. He had shown them! He had shown them what a wonder he really was!

Hildegarde Hoyt Swift

NOT LIKELY

EBENEZER NEVER-COULD-SNEEZER

He Could Not Sneeze

Ebenezer Never-Could-Sneezer was a wonderful
old French soldier. All the children in his village
loved him. He could do anything. He could
tell stories by the hour. He never seemed to begin
a story. He never seemed to end a story. But he
could tell them all the same.

All the children loved to listen to Ebenezer's stories. He told them stories of little boys and girls he had seen when he had been a soldier in Napoleon's armies.

But even though Ebenezer could do anything, and tell stories day after day, there was one thing he could not do. He could not sneeze.

You might suppose it was because he never caught cold. But no, it wasn't that. He sometimes did catch cold.

You might suppose it was because he never shook pepper in his soup. But no, it wasn't that. He sometimes did shake pepper in his soup.

Ebenezer couldn't sneeze because he had no nose to sneeze with. What! No nose! Oh dear, how did that happen?

Ebenezer had a nose when he was a baby. He had a nose when he was a small boy. He had a nose when he was a young man. He had a nose when he marched away with Napoleon's army to fight for France. He had a nose before the battle

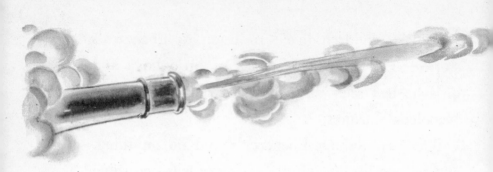

of Waterloo. But after the battle of Waterloo his nose was gone. A cannon ball came along and snipped it off.

Now the strange thing was that sometimes Ebenezer wanted to sneeze very much. Though his nose had been snipped off by a cannon ball, still, sometimes, he could feel his nose itching. And then, how he wanted to sneeze!

He could throw back his head, open his mouth, close his eyes and say, "Ah-ah-ah-," or he could say, "Ker-ker-ker," just as well as you or anyone else. But he could not say a single "Choo!" Just think of getting ready to say a good, loud "Choo!" and then not being able to say it. It made Ebenezer most unhappy.

One morning Ebenezer had what he thought was a very bright idea. He would make himself a wooden nose. In the woodpile he found just the piece of wood he needed. He made a nose out of the wood that looked like the nose he had had before the battle of Waterloo.

It was a very large nose, but Ebenezer liked that all the better. In the end of the nose he made a hole as large as the mouth of a bottle. Into this hole he fitted a cork just as you would in a bottle. He fastened his wooden nose in place, put a corkscrew in one of his pockets, and sat down in the sun to wait until he should feel like sneezing.

Very soon, Ebenezer felt a sneeze coming. He was so excited that he trembled all over. Soon he would know if his new wooden nose would work. Full of hope, he threw back his head, opened his mouth, closed his eyes, and said, "Ah-ah-ah-!"

Oh dear, oh dear, where had he put that cork-screw? In which pocket was it hiding?

As fast as his fingers could fly, he hunted in his coat pockets. The corkscrew wasn't there. And all the time he kept saying, "Ah-ah-ah-!"

Then he hunted in his other pockets. At last he found the corkscrew. Fast as he could, he screwed it into the cork in the end of his nose, and just at the end of another "Ah-ah-ah-," he gave it a quick pull and out it came with a loud "Pop!"

He tried it again. "Ah-ah-ah-pop!" "Ker-ker-ker-pop!" Well, that was something. But he could not really feel happy with an "Ah-ah-ah-pop!" or a "Ker-ker-ker-pop!" What he wanted with all his heart was a good loud "Ah-ah-ah-choo!" or a "Ker-ker-ker-choo!"

"I am afraid," he said to himself sadly, "that I shall never, never sneeze again."

So he threw away the corkscrew. He threw away the cork. He threw away the wooden nose.

A NOSE FOR EBENEZER

But even at that moment something was happening. Something was happening that was going to bring Ebenezer a happy surprise. Word came that the new railroad from Paris to the sea would run right through the village. The sleepy little town woke up and began to buzz with talk.

"A railroad! What do you think of that!" said everybody to everybody else.

"We'll have a station, too," they said. "Trains will come and go just as they do in Paris."

Buzz, buzz, buzz! How they talked. The more they talked of the railroad, the more excited they became. The Mayor began to carry a cane and wear a tall hat. The clock in the town hall was set. For the first time in fifty years it was right, and people could tell what time it was.

For months they worked on plans. For months they worked on the tracks. For months they worked on the station. Finally the day came for the first train. No one in the village had ever seen a railroad train or a railroad engine, so everyone went to the station. And of course Ebenezer was there, too.

The new station had a fresh coat of yellow paint. The new tracks went in one direction toward Paris, and in the other direction toward the sea.

The people were so excited that half of them were talking and half of them were laughing. Then the half that had been talking began to laugh, and the half that had been laughing began to talk. They were so mixed up that everyone was talking out of one side of his mouth and laughing out of the other side of his mouth at the same time. You never heard such a noise! Finally, the clock in the town hall struck eleven.

"H-ooooooo-h-ooooooo-hoo-hoo!" Right on time, the train whistled. Right on time, it appeared in sight. Right on time, it drew up at the station, bell ringing, engine puffing, brakes squeaking.

Everybody shouted. Babies screamed and dogs barked. People waved from the windows of the train. People waved from both sides of the station. Ebenezer waved both hands at once.

Rat-tat-tat down the steps of the car came the conductor's heels and the conductor with them. He bowed. He smiled. He bowed again.

He shook hands with the Mayor. He shook hands with the Mayor's new cane. He shook hands with everybody, until it was time to leave.

Oh, that was a big moment for Ebenezer! Just as the conductor shouted, "A—l-l-l aboard!" just as the engine bell began to ring, Ebenezer felt a sneeze

coming. Back flew his head. Open flew his mouth.
Tight shut his eyes.

"Ah-ah-ah-" said Ebenezer.

"Choo!" said the engine.

"Ker-ker-ker-" said Ebenezer.

"Choo!" said the engine. It was a great big
wonderful choo, the loudest choo you ever heard.

"Ah-ah-ah-choo! Ker-ker-ker-choo!" It was
the first good sneeze Ebenezer had had since
before the battle of Waterloo! He kept it up as
long as the train was in sight.

From that day on, Ebenezer saved all his sneezes for train time. He knew when every train would leave, and he never missed a train.

Ebenezer would wait until the conductor called, "A—l-l-l aboard!" He would wait until the engine bell rang. Then he would throw back his head, open his mouth, shut his eyes and say, "Ah-ah-ah-" and "Choo!" would say the engine.

"Ker-ker-ker-" he would say.

"Choo!" would say the engine.

"Ah-ah-ah-choo-choo! Ker-ker-ker-choo-choo! Ah-ker-choo! Ahkerchoo, ahkerchoo, ahkerchoo-ahkerchoo-ahkerchoo-ahkerchoo!"

There, now, if you have your breath again after all that sneezing, here's the end of it. To this very day, when the little boys and girls in that village hear the trains leaving the station, they laugh and say, "There goes Ebenezer Never-Could-Sneezer's Nose."

Gilbert S. Pattillo

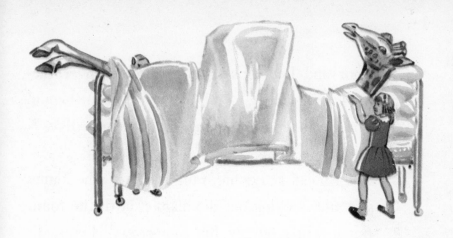

THE TAME GIRAFFE

AT HOME

Elinor and Lee were tucking the Tame Giraffe into bed. Elinor was tucking him in along the neck (it was a long job in more ways than one), and Lee was tucking in his legs. He has a bad habit of kicking when he is going to bed, which makes it hard to settle him down. Once he almost knocked Lee's front teeth out.

"I'm going to visit school tomorrow," the Tame Giraffe said suddenly, and lay very still, to see what Elinor and Lee would say to that.

Elinor and Lee looked at each other over the back of his head.

"You mean you are going, if it's a nice day?" Elinor asked.

"No, I mean I'm going, rain or shine," the Tame Giraffe said, kicking out the blanket at the bottom.

"But it won't be any fun tomorrow," Lee said, sitting on the Tame Giraffe's feet to hold them down. "We aren't having any painting tomorrow."

"Never mind," said the Tame Giraffe. "I don't care a snap for painting. I'm no good at painting myself."

"And I don't think we're even having dancing," Lee said.

"Dancing!" sniffed the Tame Giraffe, sticking his nose in the air. He stuck it up so high the blankets around his neck came out again.

"All right, get a sore throat," Elinor said, as cross as two sticks. "And you know how bad it is when you get a sore throat. A sore throat a mile long must be terrible."

214

"It is, but I won't get one, so there."

"How do you know you won't? Come on, Lee.
Let him catch cold and get a sore throat."

So Elinor and Lee went out quickly and shut
the door. Then they went over in the corner and
whispered about things.

"Oh, dear," Elinor whispered, "what are we
going to do? Miss Edwards will be wild."

"She certainly will be," Lee whispered back.
"Wild is no word for it. Let's hope he forgets
before morning."

But he didn't forget. He remembered even
before he brushed his teeth. And he didn't have
a sore throat, either.

"Goody, goody-goody," he said. "School-today, school-today, school-today."

"Oh, keep still," Lee said. "You'll hate school. There isn't a single tree in the school yard for you to eat. It's all cement."

"Goody-again," said the Tame Giraffe. "I love cement. When I run on cement, I sound like a horse. And if there is anything I'd rather be than a giraffe, it's a horse."

"Don't be silly," Lee said. "If you were a horse, we couldn't have you around the house."

"I wouldn't even be around the house," he said. "I'd be away, up and away." And the Tame Giraffe dashed for the breakfast table to drink his orange juice. Elinor was eating already.

"Silly!" Elinor said. "You can't be silly at school, I can tell you."

"Oh, can't I?" said the Tame Giraffe.

"Hurry up," Elinor said, as if she had not heard him. She knew that if the Tame Giraffe decided to be silly, nothing could stop him. "Mr. McIntyre will be here in a minute. And it takes you so long to eat."

"Not a bit longer than you," the Tame Giraffe said. "Only it takes me three times as long to swallow. I let the food take its time going down, that's all."

"Stop talking about it," Lee said. "There's Mr. McIntyre now. Wipe your mouth and hurry."

The Tame Giraffe hurried and came tripping down the steps after Elinor and Lee.

Mr. McIntyre was surprised to see him. "How do you suppose I could get this thing into the car?" he asked. "It's full of children already."

"Can't you put him on the back?" Lee asked.

"Well, we'll try," said Mr. McIntyre.

217

But the Tame Giraffe couldn't fold up small enough to ride on the back. Then they tried hanging him over the radiator, but both his nose and his feet dragged in the street. The Tame Giraffe didn't think much of that. Neither did Mr. McIntyre.

"What about leaving him at home?" Lee asked.

The Tame Giraffe spoke up. "Why can't I skip along behind?"

Mr. McIntyre said, "You can try."

So the Tame Giraffe went skipping along behind the car, and when they got to school, he went skipping through the front door without letting the teachers go in ahead. Then he went running upstairs to the classroom. Elinor and Lee wondered what Miss Edwards would say.

But Elinor and Lee had the surprise of their lives. Miss Edwards liked the Tame Giraffe on the spot.

"It's so nice to have you visit us today," she said. "I do hope he likes us, don't you, children?"

"Yes," they all said together—all except Elinor and Lee.

"Thank you," said the Tame Giraffe, in his best manner. "I am happy to be here."

"Silly again," thought Elinor.

"Fish-nets," thought Lee.

"Hmm," said the Tame Giraffe, looking at all the books on Miss Edwards's desk. "Hmm, very good work," he said, looking at all the paintings hanging on the walls.

"Thank you," said Miss Edwards. "You are from Africa, aren't you?"

"I am," said the Tame Giraffe.

"Isn't it exciting, children, to have someone from Africa visit us?" asked Miss Edwards. "We must ask him to tell us all about Africa. Shall we?"

"Yes," they all said together—all except Elinor and Lee.

At first the Tame Giraffe did not want to talk to the whole class.

"Please, do sit down," said Miss Edwards.

"Thank you," said the Tame Giraffe, and sat down in a chair near the blackboard, behind Miss Edwards's desk. He picked up a piece of chalk to be nibbling at while he listened. He always had to be nibbling at something. But Miss Edwards didn't even say a word about chalk not being good to eat.

"Let's tell the Tame Giraffe what we know about Africa," she said. "Joan, what is the name of a river in Africa?"

Joan didn't seem to be going to answer. Finally the Tame Giraffe took the wet chalk out of his mouth and made some letters on the board.

"The Nile," said Joan.

"That's right," said Miss Edwards, "though you might have been quicker. And now, Caroline, will you draw a map of Africa on the board at the back, please?"

Caroline went to the board and drew a map, but she kept looking around, because the Tame Giraffe was doing this on his board:

"Good," said Miss Edwards. "You may sit down, Caroline.

"Ellen, suppose you name some of the animals we always think of when we think of Africa."

The Tame Giraffe had to draw like the wind to keep ahead of Ellen. It was bad drawing, but you could guess what they were.

When he began to draw a giraffe, the children giggled and giggled.

"What is so funny?" Miss Edwards asked.

"Look behind you," they all shouted together—
all except Elinor and Lee.

Miss Edwards jumped because she thought it
was a mouse. But when she turned around and saw
what it really was, she laughed, too. It was lucky
Miss Edwards wasn't cross at the Tame Giraffe
for playing tricks like that.

"Isn't that clever?" she said kindly. "I never
would have thought of making a picture game
out of the lesson. Now the children will remember
the answers so much better, won't you, children?"

"We will!" they all said together—all except
Elinor and Lee.

Luckily the bell for milk-and-crackers-at-eleven
rang just then.

"You children take Mr. Giraffe up to the
lunch room," said Miss Edwards, "and see that
he gets enough to eat. I hope you can stay for
a little lunch," she said to the Tame Giraffe.
"It isn't much, but it's always a good way to see
the children."

"I should love to stay," said the Tame Giraffe. "But I must be getting home. I have so much to do this morning."

"I'm sure you have," said Miss Edwards. "Do come again when you can stay longer. We are glad you came."

"Yes, yes, come again," shouted the children— all except Elinor and Lee.

"Well, good-by," said Miss Edwards.

"Good-by," said the Tame Giraffe, and hurried downstairs to Mr. McIntyre.

Mr. McIntyre took him home all by himself inside the car. But Mr. McIntyre didn't say a word to him the whole way. Mr. McIntyre thought it was all very silly. Not that the Tame Giraffe really cared what Mr. McIntyre thought.

When the Tame Giraffe got out of the car, he said, "Miss Edwards is a wonderful teacher, but she has a lot of stupid children. Elinor and Lee never said a word the whole morning."

Lesley Frost

JUMP ROPE RHYMES

LITTLE SISTER

I had a little sister.
She dressed in pink.
She washed her dishes
In the sink.
How many dishes did she break?
One, two, three, - - - - - - - etc.

H-o-p.
Try to catch me!

*(Those turning the rope change the speed to make the one
who is jumping trip or miss.)*

Mrs. Brown
Went up to town.
She gave me a nickel
To buy me a pickle;
The pickle was sour.
She gave me a flower;
The flower was yellow.
She gave me a fellow;
The fellow was lazy.
She gave me a slap;
The slap was hard.
She gave me a card;
On this card—said,

Spanish dancer does a high kick.
Spanish dancer does a low split.
Spanish dancer does a low bow.
Spanish dancer, that'll do now.

(*Fit actions to words, and then run out.*)

LADY MOON

Lady moon, lady moon,
Turn 'round, 'round, 'round.
Lady moon, lady moon,
Touch ground, ground, ground.
Lady moon, lady moon,
Show your shoe, shoe, shoe.
Lady moon, lady moon,
Let that do, do, do.

(The person jumping must do each of the things the rhyme says without tripping. At the end she must run out.)

CHARLIE CHAPLIN

Charlie Chaplin went to France
To show the French girls how to dance.
First on the heel,
And then on the toe,
'Round and about and out you go.
(*Act this one out.*)

TEDDY BEAR

Teddy bear, Teddy bear,
Say your prayers, prayers, prayers.
Teddy bear, Teddy bear,
Climb upstairs, stairs, stairs.
Teddy bear, Teddy bear,
Go to sleep, sleep, sleep.
Teddy bear, Teddy bear,
Don't you peep, peep, peep.
(*Jump as many times as possible with your eyes closed.*)

COLLECTED BY *Lucy Nulton*

THE GHOST OF A PIRATE

A Strange Laugh

Allan sat on a huge rock and counted his shells. He had been picking them up all afternoon, and his pockets were nearly bursting.

"They are good ones, too," he said to himself. "The boys will be glad to see these shells when I get back to the city. I'll take them to school in the fall."

He put all the shells out on the rock. Some of them were as big as his hand, and others were as small as his little fingernail. He was too busy to see a little girl who walked across the beach toward him.

"Have you any shells from the cave?" she asked suddenly.

Allan jumped. "Why, I thought I was the only one here," he cried.

The little girl laughed. "I'm the only other one," she said. "The beach is lonely today. Where do you come from?"

"Well, I live in the city," Allan answered.

"But my mother and I are staying at the white house over there. We're going to be here for two weeks."

The little girl pushed her bangs out of her eyes. "We live here all the time," she said, "down at the big farm. My name is Mary, and I'm eight and a half." Then she asked her first question again. "Have you any shells from the cave? They are the best ones."

"Why should they be any better than these?" asked Allan. "These are good ones."

"Yes, but the others are better because they are so old," said Mary. "They are very old. A man came all the way across the country just to look at them."

"Then they must be good ones," cried Allan. "Do you know where the cave is?"

"Of course I do," answered Mary. "Come on. I'll show you."

Allan followed her along the beach. It was a much longer walk than he thought it would be.

They went farther and farther. At last they came to the high rocks that they were looking for. On one side the waves beat against the shore, and on the other side the rocks rose like a great wall.

The gulls built their nests on these rocks, and they didn't like to have children coming so close to them. They flew around and around, screaming. It seemed to Allan as if they called out, "Go back! Go back!"

Mary led the way through a small opening in the rocks, and there they were, inside a long, dark cave. It was such a big cave that they couldn't see where it ended.

"It's really a huge cave," Mary said. "It goes back ever so far. They say pirates used to hide here."

"It would be a good place for a pirate's den," cried Allan.

"What about the ghosts of pirates?" asked Mary. "It would be a fine place for them, too."

She had hardly spoken when a queer voice from the back of the cave called, "Al, Al!"

"Who is that?" cried Allan.

"I–I don't know," said Mary.

"Al," called the voice, louder than before.

Allan took hold of Mary's arm. "It's calling me," he cried. "It's calling my name! What shall I do?"

Mary had already turned toward the mouth of the cave.

"Let's go home," she said.

Allan was quite ready. "It's supper time, anyway," he said. "And it's too late to see anything." He hoped Mary would not think that he was frightened.

Just as they were climbing out of the cave, the voice called out a third time, "Al, Al!"

Allan looked behind him quickly. "What do you want?" he called back.

There was no answer, but way inside the cave, the children could hear a loud laugh. It

was not a pleasant laugh. It was a very frightening
one. It was the most frightening sound the children
had ever heard.

"It's a ghost," said Mary in a wobbly voice.
Off she went, over the rocks and down the beach.
Allan ran after her as fast as his legs would carry
him.

In the Cave

The next morning Allan couldn't keep from thinking about the cave. It seemed silly to have been frightened, now that the hot sun was beating down on his head.

"Besides, there are no such things as ghosts," he said to himself. "Why should I be afraid? I'll go back to the cave and get some shells. That will show Mary that I'm not afraid of a silly old ghost."

He started off down the beach, whistling as he walked. Even the gulls seemed more friendly in the bright sunlight. When Allan reached the mouth of the cave, he stopped to listen. Except for the waves beating on the shore behind him, there was not a sound. He went slowly into the cave.

236

It was dark inside. It seemed even darker than it was, because his eyes were used to the sunlight. He put his hands on the rocky wall, and felt his way along.

The cave was very quiet. He almost laughed at the idea of a pirate's ghost hiding there. But as he turned to go outside again, he felt something go past him. It went softly and quietly. Allan shivered. Someone else was in the cave then. He was afraid to move.

Once again it passed by, touching his arm, and then from the back of the cave came that ugly laugh. Allan screamed and started to run. He didn't stop until he was way up the beach and saw Mary coming toward him.

"Where are you going?" asked Mary. "You seem to be in a hurry."

He told her what had happened.

Mary nodded. "Ghosts," she said.

"My mother says there aren't any ghosts," cried Allan.

"Well," Mary said, "it certainly sounded like a ghost yesterday. If we could see it we would know what it really is."

"I suppose we would," answered Allan.

"My father has a huge flashlight that he takes when he goes fishing," said Mary. "I'll ask him to let us take it to the cave."

"I'll go with you to get the flashlight," he said.

Mary looked at him. "You are not afraid, are you?" she asked.

"Not—not very," he answered.

But when they had taken the flashlight into the cave, he said, "Let's flash it right now."

"No," Mary answered softly. "The thing may not come if it sees the light. I'll be ready to flash it quickly."

They waited and waited. Everything was quiet.

"I'm tired," Allan said at last. "I think we've been here for hours."

Mary sighed. "I'm tired, too," she said. "Shall we give up?"

"Ha-ha-ha," laughed a voice. It was right behind them.

"Hurry!" cried Allan. "Turn it on."

In another minute Mary flashed the light on the rocks behind them. There sat the strangest bird Allan had ever seen. It was a big bird, and it had a huge beak with bright-colored stripes.

Mary burst out laughing. "It's only a puffin," she said. "To think we were afraid of a puffin!"

The bird blinked at her. "Al," it called. "Al."

"Here I am, Mr. Puffin," Allan answered. "Do you mind if we take a few shells from your rocks?"

The puffin said nothing.

"He's a funny bird," Allan said. "I never saw one like him before."

"He's the ghost of a pirate," laughed Mary. "I wonder if all ghosts turn out to be puffins."

Robin Palmer

THERE ONCE WAS A PUFFIN

Oh, there once was a Puffin,
Just the shape of a muffin,
And he lived on an island
In the
    bright
        blue sea!

He ate little fishes,
That were most delicious,
And he had them for supper
And he
    had them
        for tea.

But this poor little Puffin,
He couldn't play nothin',
For he hadn't anybody
To play
    with
        at all.

So he sat on his island,
And he cried for awhile, and
He felt very lonely,
And he

      felt

          very small.

Then along came the fishes,
And they said, "If you wishes,
You can have us for playmates,
Instead of

      for

          tea!"

So now they play together,
In all sorts of weather,
And the Puffin eats pancakes,
Like you

      and

          like me.

Florence Page Jaques

WISE ANIMALS

THE TORTOISE AND
THE ELEPHANT

One day an elephant met a tortoise, and the tortoise said, "What sort of little beast is that?"

"What! Little beast? Do you dare to call me a little beast?" said the elephant.

"Well, who are you, then, if you aren't a little beast?" asked the tortoise.

244

"I'm the biggest of all the beasts in the whole forest," answered the elephant.

"The biggest of all the beasts in the forest?" said the tortoise. "But I could jump over you if I liked!"

"You? Jump over me?" said the elephant. "You just try!"

"Very well, I will try it. Only today I am a bit tired. I have walked a long way. Come tomorrow to this same place, and you'll see that I can jump over you!"

"Right," said the elephant. "I'll be here!"

The next day the tortoise and the elephant met again at the same place.

Now the tortoise, as you know, is a clever creature. She had asked her sister to come, too, and hide in the grass. And the elephant said, "Well, Miss Tortoise, are you going to start jumping?"

"I am!" she answered. "You just stand quite still, and I'll jump from this side over to the other!"

245

The elephant stood still, and the tortoise made believe that she was going to jump. All this time her sister was hiding in the grass on the other side.

"Look out!" shouted the tortoise. "Hop!"

At that the elephant turned round to the other side, and there was the tortoise's sister poking her head out of the grass and saying, "Here I am!"

The elephant was greatly surprised and said, "Well, now, jump back again!"

"All right!" answered the tortoise. "Hop!"

The elephant turned round again and there was the tortoise back just where it was before. The elephant was still more surprised, and said, "Well, really, you are good at jumping. Let's see you do it again!"

"Hop!" cried the tortoise. The elephant turned round, and there was the tortoise again on the other side.

"Once again!" he shouted.

"Hop!" cried the tortoise, and again appeared in the same place as before.

The elephant had no idea the tortoise was so clever at jumping, and he said, "I can see you are very good at jumping, but of course you cannot run so fast as I. Running is quite another matter! And you certainly cannot run at all. In fact, I should say you're the slowest of all the beasts in the world!"

"Ha, ha!" laughed the tortoise. "You don't know me at all! I can run a race with anybody and win!"

"Very well," said the elephant. "Let's have a race as far as that tree over there!"

"It's all very well for you!" answered the tortoise. "You haven't been jumping! I have, and I'm quite tired. Come along tomorrow, and then we'll have a running race. You'll see that I can beat you!"

The next day the tortoise called together her relatives, all her brothers and sisters, all her uncles and aunts, and said to them, "Go and hide in the grass between here and that tree over there."

248

And all the tortoise's relatives went and hid in the grass.

Soon the elephant came up and said, "Well, Miss Tortoise, are we going to run our race?"

"Of course! Why not?" she answered. "You just stand beside me!"

They went and stood side by side.

"Ready! Go!" cried the tortoise, and the elephant started off, running, but the tortoise hid herself in the grass. The elephant went on running, running, and thought, "Well, I must have left the tortoise a long way behind by now!"

Then he stopped and shouted, "Miss Tortoise, Miss Tortoise, where are you?"

Her brother answered from out of the grass, "Here I am! Why have you stopped?"

Then the elephant started off running again. He ran and ran, and at last he stopped and asked, "Where are you, Miss Tortoise?"

And the tortoise's aunt answered from out of the grass, "Here I am! Why don't you go on running?"

The elephant saw that the tortoise kept ahead of him all the time, so he tried as hard as he could and ran on as fast as he was able.

At last he got to the tree and thought, "Well, now I must surely be ahead of her! Where are you, Miss Tortoise?" he asked.

And the tortoise's uncle answered from out of the grass, "I've been waiting for you here a long time!"

The elephant was more surprised than ever and said to himself, "Well, that's some tortoise!" and went home very angry.

Valery Carrick

THE ELEPHANT AND
THE WHALE

One day a hare and a jackal set off to travel together. After a while they came to the shore of the sea, and there they saw an elephant standing and talking to a whale.

The elephant said, "Look here, Brother Whale, you are the strongest beast in the sea, and I'm the strongest in the forest. Why should we not rule all the other beasts? You rule those in the water, and I will rule those on land. If anyone doesn't do as we say, we'll wipe him off the face of the earth."

"Right," answered the whale. "We will."

251

The jackal was frightened when he heard this, and said to the hare, "Do you hear what they are saying? We must run or we shall get into trouble for having listened to what they were saying."

But the hare said, "What are you afraid of? Do you really believe they can rule over everyone else just because they are big and strong? Just you watch and see me make fools of them."

Then the hare got a long rope, took one end, and went up to the elephant and said to him, "Sir, you are big and strong, and I'm told you are very kind, too! Please help me, for I'm in great trouble! My cow was eating quietly, when she sank down into the marsh, and I am unable to pull her out!"

The elephant was pleased at being called strong and kind, and said, "Of course, I'll be only too glad to help you, Mr. Hare! Tell me where your cow is."

"She's deep in the marsh," answered the hare. "You can't see her. You can only see her two horns sticking out! I'll go and fasten the other end of the rope to her horns. When I start beating the drum, you start pulling."

"All right," said the elephant. "Go and fasten the rope."

Then the hare took the other end of the rope, and went off to the whale, and said, "Oh, Mr. Whale! There's no fish in the sea, no beast in the forest, no bird in the air, as strong as you are. Please help me!"

The whale was very much pleased at being told he was greater than all the other beasts and birds, and he said, "Certainly I will help you! What is the matter?"

"My cow was quietly eating," said the hare, "when she sank in the marsh! I tried and tried to get her out, but it was no use! Please be kind and help me out of my trouble! Here's a rope. You take one end, and I'll fasten the other end to the cow's horns. Then, when I start beating the drum, you start pulling. You're sure to pull her out!"

253

"Right!" answered the whale. "I will!"

Then the hare went off. He stopped halfway between the two, and started beating the drum. The elephant began to pull, and the whale began to pull! First they pulled quite gently, and the rope just got tight. They then began to pull harder, and the rope got tighter and tighter.

"How very surprising!" thought the elephant.
"Surely that cow can't have sunk so deep that I
can't pull her out!"

He tried harder, and started pulling the whale
toward the shore.

And the whale thought, "Well, this hare must
have a very large cow! Surely I shall be able to
pull her out! If I don't, all the beasts will start
making fun of me!"

Once more the whale pulled and this time he pulled the elephant right up to the shore.

"Well, I never! Is that you, Brother Elephant?" he asked.

"Well, I never! Is that you, Brother Whale?" answered the elephant.

"Well, a pretty pair of fools the hare has made of us!" they said together. "Where is that hare?"

But Mr. Hare had gone.

Valery Carrick

TAKE AWAY ONE

Five little monkeys,
    Swinging from a tree;
Teasing Uncle Crocodile,
    Merry as can be;
Swinging high, swinging low,
    Swinging left and right.
"Dear Uncle Crocodile,
    Come and take a bite!"

Four little monkeys,
    Sitting in the tree;
Heads down, tails down,
    Dreary as can be.
Weeping loud, weeping low,
    Crying to each other:
"Wicked Uncle Crocodile,
    To gobble up our brother!"

Laura E. Richards

THE MONKEY AND THE CROCODILE

THE FIRST TRICK

In a great tree on a river bank lived a Monkey. In the river there were many Crocodiles.

A Crocodile watched the Monkey for a long time, and one day she said to her son, "My son, get one of those Monkeys for me. I want the heart of a Monkey to eat."

"How am I to catch a Monkey?" asked the little Crocodile. "I do not travel on land, and the Monkey does not go into the water."

"Put your wits to work, and you'll find a way," said the mother.

The little Crocodile thought and thought.

At last he said to himself, "I know what I'll do.

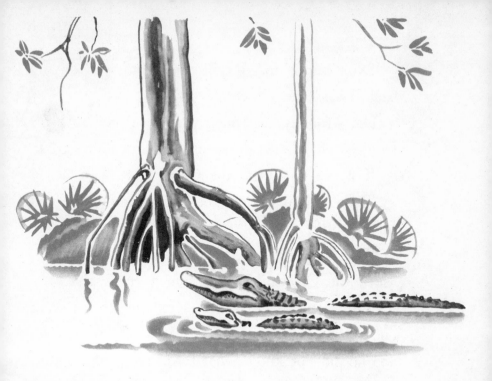

I'll get that Monkey that lives in a big tree on the river bank. He wishes to go across the river to the island where the fruit is so ripe."

So the Crocodile swam to the tree where the Monkey lived. But he was a stupid Crocodile.

"Oh, Monkey," he called, "come with me over to the island where the fruit is so ripe."

"How can I go with you?" asked the Monkey. "I do not swim."

"No—but I do. I will take you over on my back," said the Crocodile.

The Monkey was hungry, and wanted the ripe fruit, so he jumped down on the Crocodile's back.

"Off we go!" said the Crocodile.

"This is a fine ride you are giving me!" said the Monkey.

"Do you think so? Well, how do you like this?" asked the Crocodile, going under the water.

"Oh, don't!" cried the Monkey, as he went under the water, too. He was afraid to let go, and he did not know what to do under the water.

When the Crocodile came up, the Monkey asked, "Why did you take me under water, Crocodile?"

"I am going to kill you by keeping you under water," answered the Crocodile. "My mother wants Monkey-heart to eat, and I'm going to take yours to her."

"I wish you had told me," said the Monkey. "Then I might have brought it with me."

"How queer!" said the stupid Crocodile. "Do you mean to say that you left your heart back there in the tree?"

"That is what I mean," said the Monkey. "If you want my heart, we must go back to the tree and get it. But we are so near the island where the ripe fruit is, please take me there first."

"No, Monkey," said the Crocodile, "I'll take you straight back to your tree. Never mind the ripe fruit. Get your heart and bring it to me at once. Then we'll see about going to the island."

"Very well," said the Monkey.

But no sooner had he jumped onto the bank of the river than up he ran into the tree.

From the top of the tree he called down to the Crocodile, "My heart is way up here! If you want it, come for it, come for it!"

The Second Trick

The Monkey soon moved away from that tree. He wanted to get away from the Crocodile.

But the Crocodile found him, far down the river, living in another tree.

In the middle of the river was an island covered with fruit trees.

Half way between the bank of the river and the island, a large rock rose out of the water. The Monkey could jump to the rock, and then to the island. The Crocodile watched the Monkey crossing from the bank of the river to the rock, and then to the island.

He thought to himself, "The Monkey will stay on the island all day, and I'll catch him on his way home at night."

The Monkey ate and ate of the ripe fruit, while the Crocodile swam about, watching him all day.

Toward night the Crocodile crawled out of the water and lay quite still on the rock.

When it grew dark among the trees, the Monkey started for home. He ran down to the river bank, and there he stopped.

"What is the matter with the rock?" the Monkey thought to himself. "I never saw it so high before. Oh, the Crocodile is lying on it!"

He went to the edge of the water and called, "Hello, Rock!"

No answer.

Then he called again, "Hello, Rock!"

No answer.

Three times the Monkey called, and then he said, "Why is it, Friend Rock, that you do not answer me tonight?"

"Oh," said the stupid Crocodile to himself, "the rock answers the Monkey at night. I'll have to answer for the rock this time."

So he answered, "Yes, Monkey, what is it?"

The Monkey laughed, and said, "Oh, it's you, Crocodile, is it?"

"Yes," said the Crocodile. "I am waiting here for you. I am going to eat you."

"You have caught me this time," said the Monkey. "There is no other way for me to go home. Open your mouth wide so that I can jump right into it."

Now the Monkey well knew that when Crocodiles open their mouths wide, they shut their eyes.

While the Crocodile lay on the rock with his mouth wide open and his eyes shut, the Monkey jumped.

But not into his mouth! Oh, no! He landed on the top of the Crocodile's head, and then sprang quickly to the bank and up into his tree.

When the Crocodile saw the trick the Monkey had played on him, he said, "Monkey, you are very clever. You are not afraid. I'll let you alone after this."

"Thank you, Crocodile, but I shall be on the watch for you just the same," said the Monkey.

Ellen C. Babbitt

THE TAME SWAN TALKS TO
THE WILD SWAN

Wild Swan, Wild Swan,
Yonder in the sky,
Wild Swan, Wild Swan,
Floating swiftly by;

You and I are kinsfolk,
You and I are brothers;
Alike are our wings,
Alike are our feathers.

Alike are our long necks,
Growing white and tall,
Alike are our webbed feet,
Yellow-gray and small.

Both of us are brothers,
Both of us the same;
But you have a wild heart,
And my heart is tame.

Kathryn Worth

267

GRANNY'S BLACKIE

Once upon a time a rich man gave a baby Elephant to a woman. She took the best of care of this great baby and soon became very fond of him.

The children in the village called her Granny, and they called the Elephant "Granny's Blackie."

The Elephant carried the children on his back all over the village. They gave him some of their food and he played with them.

"Please, Blackie, give us a swing," they said to him almost every day.

"Come on! Who is first?" Blackie answered, and picked them up with his trunk, swung them high in the air, and then put them down again, carefully.

But Blackie never did any work.

He ate and slept, played with the children, and visited with Granny.

One day Blackie wanted Granny to go off to the woods with him.

"I can't go, Blackie, dear. I have too much work to do!"

Then Blackie looked at her and saw that she was growing old and tired.

"I am young and strong," he thought. "I'll see if I cannot find some work to do. If I could bring some money home to her, she would not have to work so hard."

So next morning, bright and early, he started down to the river bank.

There he found a man who was in great trouble. There was a long line of wagons so heavily loaded that the oxen could not pull them across the river.

When the man saw Blackie standing on the bank, he asked, "Who owns this Elephant? I want to hire him to help my oxen pull these wagons across the river."

A child standing near by said, "That is Granny's Blackie."

"Very well," said the man, "I'll pay two pieces of silver for each wagon this Elephant pulls across the river."

Blackie was glad to hear this. He went into the river, and pulled one wagon after another across to the other side.

Then he went up to the man for the money.

The man counted out one piece of silver for each wagon.

When Blackie saw that the man had counted out but one piece of silver for each wagon, instead of two, he would not touch the money at all. He stood in the road and would not let the wagons pass him.

The man tried to get Blackie out of the way, but not one step would he move.

Then the man went back and counted out another piece of silver for each of the wagons and put the silver in a bag tied around Blackie's neck.

Then Blackie started for home, proud to think that he had a present for Granny.

The children had missed Blackie and had asked Granny where he was, but she said she did not know where he had gone.

They all looked for him but it was nearly night before they heard him coming.

"Where have you been, Blackie? And what is that around your neck?" the children cried, running to meet their friend.

But Blackie would not stop to talk with his friends. He ran straight home to Granny.

"Oh, Blackie," she said, "where have you been? What is in that bag?" Then she took the bag off his neck and looked inside.

"Oh, Blackie, Blackie," said Granny, "how hard you must have worked to earn these pieces of silver! What a good Blackie you are!"

And after that Blackie did all the hard work and Granny rested, and they were both very happy.

Ellen C. Babbitt

FOOLISH PEOPLE

THE GOOD FLEA AND
THE WICKED KING

Once upon a time there was a wicked king who made his people very unhappy. Everybody hated him, and wanted to get rid of him. But how? He was the strongest. He was the king. Whenever he was told that his people were not happy, he said, "Well, what of it? I don't care a rap!"

Every day he became a little more wicked than the day before. This set a little flea to thinking. It was a little bit of a flea, but a good flea. It was not like most fleas, for it had been very well brought up. It bit people only when it was hungry.

"What if I were to do something about this?" it said to itself. "Perhaps I can make the king see how wicked he is. It is not without danger. But no matter—I will try."

That night the wicked king, after having done all sorts of wicked things that day, was going to sleep when he felt what seemed to be the point of a pin.

Bite!

The king turned over on the other side.

Bite! Bite! Bite!

"Who is it that bites me so?" cried the king in a loud voice.

"It is I," said a very little voice.

"You? Who are you?"

"A little flea who wishes to make you see how wicked you are."

"A flea? Just you wait! Just you wait, and you shall see!"

And the king sprang from his bed and shook the sheets. But the good flea had hidden itself in the king's hair.

"Ah," said the king, "it has gone now, and I shall be able to go to sleep."

He had hardly put his head down on the pillow, when—

Bite!

"How? What? Again?"

Bite! Bite!

"You dare to come back, you wicked little flea! Think for a moment what you are doing! You are no bigger than a grain of sand, and you dare to bite one of the greatest kings on earth!"

"Well, what of it? I don't care a rap!" answered the flea in the very words of the king.

"Ah, if I only had you in my hand!"

"Yes, but you haven't!"

The wicked king did not sleep all that night, and the next morning he was very angry. He wanted to kill the good little flea. By his orders,

they cleaned the palace from top to bottom. His bed was made by ten old women who could catch fleas. But they caught nothing, for the good flea had hidden itself under the collar of the king's coat.

That night the king, who was worn out for want of sleep, lay back on both his ears, though this is said to be hard to do. He had hardly put out his light, when he felt the flea on his neck.

Bite! Bite!

"What is this?"

"It is I—the flea of yesterday."

"But what do you want?"

"I wish you to make your people happy."

"Ho, there, my soldiers! Ho, there, everybody! The whole lot of you! Come catch this flea!"

The whole lot of them came in. The king was angry. He made everybody tremble. He was angry with everybody in the palace. They were all afraid. All this time, the flea kept itself hidden in the king's nightcap. The soldiers could not find him.

The king could not lie down, even on the grass, without being bitten. The good flea did not let him sleep a single minute.

Bite! Bite!

It would take too long to tell how often the king slapped himself in trying to kill the flea. As he could not sleep, he grew thinner and thinner.

At last he made up his mind to do what the good flea asked.

"I will do what you wish," he said, when the flea began to bite him again.

"So much the better," answered the flea.

"What must I do?"

"Make your people happy!"

"I do not know how."

"Nothing could be more easy. You have only to go away."

"Taking my money with me?"

"Without taking anything."

"But I shall die if I have no money," said the king.

"Well, what of it? I don't care a rap!" answered the flea.

But the flea had a kind heart, and it let the king fill his pockets with money before he went away. And the people were very happy without the king.

Victor Hugo

MOLLY WHUPPIE

The Wicked Giant

Once upon a time there was a man and his wife who were not very rich. They had so many children that they couldn't find enough for all of them to eat. So they took the three youngest girls out to the forest one day, and left them there.

Now the two older girls cried a bit and felt afraid. But the youngest, whose name was Molly Whuppie, was brave and clever. She told her sisters not to give up hope. So they set off through the forest, and walked and walked and walked, but they saw no houses. It began to grow dark, and the sisters were very hungry. Even Molly Whuppie began to think of supper. At last they saw a big light, shining far away. When they came near, they saw that it came from a huge window in a huge house.

"It may be a giant's house," said the two older girls, trembling with fear.

"I mean to have my supper even if there are two giants in it," said Molly Whuppie, and knocked boldly at a huge door.

It was opened by the giant's wife. She shook her head when Molly Whuppie asked for food and a place to sleep for the night.

"You wouldn't thank me for it," she said. "My man is a giant, and when he comes home, he will be sure to kill you."

"But if you give us supper now," said clever Molly, "we shall have finished it before the giant comes home."

Now the giant's wife was not unkind. Besides, she had three daughters of her own. So she took the girls in and gave them each a bowl of bread and milk. They had hardly begun to eat before the door burst open, and a terrible giant came in.

"What have you there, wife?" asked the giant.

"See for yourself," said the giant's wife, trying to make the best of it. "They are only three poor little girls like our little girls. Now be a good giant and don't touch them."

Now this giant was not at all a good giant. He was really a wicked giant. But he only said that as they had come, they might stay all night, since they could sleep with his three daughters.

After he had had his supper, he was quite pleasant. He twisted chains of straw for the little girls to wear around their necks, but he put gold chains around his daughters' necks. Then he wished them all pleasant dreams and sent them to bed.

Now Molly Whuppie, the youngest of the three girls, was not only brave, she was clever. So when she was in bed, she lay awake and thought, and thought, and thought. At last, when everyone else was asleep, she got up softly. She took off her own and her sisters' straw chains and put them around the necks of the giant's daughters. Then she put the gold chains around her own and her sisters' necks.

Even then she did not go to sleep. She lay still and waited to see if she was really clever. She was! For in the very middle of the night, when

everybody else was sound asleep, in came the giant, very quietly. He felt for the straw chains and twisted them tight around the girls' necks. He pulled the girls out of bed, and pushed them down into his cellar. Then he went back to his own bed, thinking he had been very clever.

But he was not so clever as Molly Whuppie. At once she woke her sisters. She told them to be quiet and follow her. They slipped out of the giant's house, and ran, and ran, and ran.

When morning came, they found themselves before another great house. It was on an island in the middle of a pond. The only way they could reach it was by crossing the Bridge of One Hair.

Now Molly's sisters were afraid to try it. They said that the house might be another giant's house, and they wanted to keep away.

"Let's try," said Molly Whuppie, laughing, and over the Bridge of One Hair she ran, before you could say knife. And, after all, it was not a giant's house, but a king's castle. Molly went in and told her story to the king.

The king said, "You are a clever girl, Molly Whuppie, and you did very well. But if you can do still better and steal the giant's sword, I'll tell you what I will do. I will marry your oldest sister to my oldest son."

Well! Molly Whuppie thought this would be very fine indeed for her sister, so she said she would try.

286

THE GIANT'S SWORD

So that evening, Molly ran across the Bridge of One Hair, and ran, and ran, until she came to the giant's house. She slipped quietly into the house, crept up to the giant's room, and hid under the bed.

By and by, the giant came home, ate a huge supper, and came up the stairs to his bed. Molly kept very still and held her breath. Soon the giant began to snore. Then Molly crept out from under the bed. Quietly she crept up on the bed. Carefully she crept past his great snoring face. Quietly and carefully she took the sword that hung above the bed. But alas! the sword rattled. The noise woke the giant. Up he jumped and ran after Molly, who ran as she had never run before.

He ran, and she ran, and they both ran, until they came to the Bridge of One Hair. She hurried over it, but the giant couldn't. He was too heavy.

So he stopped and called after her, "Woe to you,
Molly Whuppie! Don't you dare to come again!"

Molly laughed at the giant.

"Twice yet," she called, "will I come to Spain!"

So Molly gave the sword to the king, and his
oldest son was married to her oldest sister.

After that, the king said again to Molly Whuppie,
"You're a clever girl, Molly, and you have done
very well. If you can do still better and steal the

giant's purse, I will marry my second son to your second sister. But you need to be careful, for the giant sleeps with the purse under his pillow!"

Well! Molly Whuppie thought this would be fine, indeed, for her second sister, so she said she would try.

THE GIANT'S PURSE

So that evening, just at sunset, Molly ran over the Bridge of One Hair, and ran, and ran, and ran, until she came to the giant's house. She slipped quietly into the house, crept up to the giant's room, and crept under the giant's bed. By and by, the giant came home. He ate a huge supper, came upstairs, and soon fell asleep, snoring.

Then Molly Whuppie slipped out from under the bed. She reached out her hand, slipped it under the pillow, and got hold of the purse. But the giant's head was so heavy on it that she had to pull and pull. When at last it came out, she fell

backward on the floor. The purse opened, and some of the money fell out with a crash. The noise woke the giant, and Molly had only time to pick up the money, when he was after her.

Then he ran, and she ran, and they both ran. At last Molly reached the Bridge of One Hair. With the purse in one hand, the money in the other, she ran across it while the giant cried, "Woe to you, Molly Whuppie! Don't you dare to come again!"

She laughed at him. "Yet once more," she called, "will I come to Spain."

So she took the purse to the king, and his second son was married to Molly's second sister.

After that the king said to her, "Molly, you are the most clever girl in the world. If you will get the ring from the giant's finger, I will give you my youngest son for yourself."

Now Molly thought the king's youngest son was the nicest young prince she had ever seen, so she said she would try.

THE GIANT'S RING

That evening, Molly hurried across the Bridge of One Hair as light as a feather. She ran, and ran, and ran, until she came to the giant's house. She slipped into the house, went upstairs, and crept under the bed. Just as before, the giant came in and ate his supper. Then he went up to bed, and snored. Oh! He snored louder than ever.

Molly crept out and reached over the bed. But no sooner had she managed to pull off the giant's ring than—oh, my!

He had her fast by the hand. He sat up in bed and said, "Molly Whuppie, you are a clever girl! Now, if I had been as wicked to you as you have been to me, what would you do to me?"

Molly thought for a moment and then she said, "I'd put you in a sack, and I'd put the cat inside with you, and I'd put the dog inside with you, and I'd put a needle and thread and a pair of shears inside with you, and I'd hang you up on a nail.

Then I'd go to the forest and cut the biggest stick I could get, and come home and take you down and bang you until you were dead!"

"Well, Molly," cried the giant, "that's just what I'll do to you!"

So he got a sack and put Molly into it with the dog and the cat and the needle and thread and the shears, and hung her on a nail in the wall. Then he went out to the forest to cut a big stick.

After he had gone, Molly Whuppie began to laugh like anything, and the dog barked and the cat mewed.

Now the giant's wife was sitting in the next room, and when she heard the noise she asked, "Whatever is the matter?"

"Nothing," answered Molly Whuppie from inside the sack, laughing like anything. "Ho, ho! Ha, ha! If you saw what I see, you would laugh, too. Ho, ho! Ha, ha!"

"What do you see, Molly?" asked the giant's wife.

But Molly never said a word except, "Ho, ho! Ha, ha! If you could see what I see!"

At last the giant's wife asked Molly to let her see. So Molly took the shears and cut a hole in the sack. Then she jumped out, helped the giant's wife in, and sewed up the hole!

Now, just at that very moment, the giant came in. Molly had hardly time enough to hide behind

the door before he rushed at the sack, pulled it down, and began to beat it with a huge tree he had cut in the forest.

"Stop! Stop!" cried his wife.

But he couldn't hear, for the dog barked and the cat mewed. Just then Molly went running off with the ring and the giant saw her.

Well, he threw down the tree and ran after her. He ran, and she ran, and they both ran, until they came to the Bridge of One Hair. And then, once more, Molly Whuppie ran over the bridge, light as a feather, but the giant had to stand on the other side. "Woe to you, Molly Whuppie!" he cried. "Don't you dare to come again!"

And she laughed at the giant. "Never more," she called, "will I come to Spain."

So she took the ring to the king, and she and the king's youngest son were married, and no one ever saw the wicked giant again.

Flora Annie Steel

294

PEKKA AND THE ROGUES

Pekka and his father lived in a little hut in the country. They had a small piece of land and two cows. They did well when the grass was green and thick, but a year came when the grass did not grow well. They couldn't cut enough hay to feed both their cows through the winter. Then the old man said, "Here we have two cows, and not enough hay to feed one. We must sell one cow, and then we can buy hay to feed the other."

So, early one morning, Pekka set off to market with the oldest cow. Pekka had never been to town before, and as he came to the market-place he walked slowly, staring at everything.

Two young rogues saw him coming along, and thought they would play a trick on him.

"Hello," they shouted at him. "Where are you going with that goat?"

Pekka stared at them, but said nothing. He knew they were making fun of him because his cow was so old and thin.

The two rogues slipped round the corner, changed their caps, and put their hands in their pockets. Then they called to him again.

"Hello, young man, how much will you take for that goat?"

Pekka stared again, but did not see that they were the same two rogues. He thought to himself, "This is our old cow all right. Why does everyone in town call her a goat?"

Soon he saw the two rogues again, and this time they called, "Listen, young man! Is that goat for sale?"

Pekka was so mixed up that he hardly knew what to answer. He said, "This isn't a goat. It's our old cow."

"You must be crazy," said the two strangers. "Of course it's a goat, and a pretty poor goat at that."

Poor Pekka was so mixed up that he let them have the cow for the price of a goat. But as he watched them driving the old cow on toward the market, he knew he had been tricked. He said to himself, "I'll follow those two and see what they do."

Pekka stood among the crowd in the market-place and watched. The two rogues soon sold his cow, old and thin as it was, for a good price. This made Pekka so angry that he made up his mind to make the two rogues pay him for the trick they had played.

So he went to the nearest inn, gave the innkeeper some money, and said, "I'm going to bring two friends to have dinner here. When we are ready to leave, I shall whirl my cap around on my finger and ask you, 'Is everything paid for?' and you must answer 'Yes.' "

"Certainly I'll say 'Yes,' " said the innkeeper. "Here is the money right in my hand."

Pekka went to two other inns, and made the same bargain at each. Then he hurried off to find the two men who had tricked him.

As soon as he found them, he said, "You gave me a good price for my goat, and now I want to do something for you. Come along and have dinner with me."

The rogues were surprised, but they thought Pekka must be even more stupid than they had supposed. So they slapped him on the back and went off with him, arm in arm.

The three ate and drank, and when they were ready to leave, Pekka stood up, whirled his cap around on his finger, and shouted to the innkeeper, "Is everything paid for?"

"Certainly, sir," said the innkeeper, and bowed politely.

The two rogues looked at each other. This was indeed wonderful. They decided to keep close to Pekka and see what would happen next.

After walking about for a while, Pekka said, "Let's go into this inn here and see what they have."

The two rogues followed him in, and when they had finished, Pekka stood up and whirled his cap.

"Is everything paid for?" he called to the innkeeper.

"Yes, sir! Glad to see you again, sir."

The two rogues looked at each other again. They could hardly believe their ears.

"Why don't you pay for what you eat and drink as other people do?" they asked.

Pekka said, "Well, it's like this. It's because of my cap. When I whirl the cap around on my finger and ask, 'Is everything paid for?' the answer is always 'Yes.' "

"What will you take for that cap?" asked the rogues.

300

"Take for it? I wouldn't dream of selling it," said Pekka. "I earn my living by it, as you can see."

"But we'll give you a good price."

"I'd rather keep the cap."

By this time they had come to another inn, and Pekka said, "Come on, and we'll have something to eat in here. You'll see that it always works."

They went into the third inn, and everything happened as before. They ate and drank, Pekka whirled his cap, and the innkeeper bowed and smiled.

When they were in the street again, the rogues made up their minds to get that cap, pay what they might. "We'll give you all our money for that cap," they said.

"How about that gold watch you have?" said Pekka.

"You can have the watch, too."

"But then I'd have no cap to wear."

"Take one of our caps."

Pekka chose the best cap, tried it on, and gave them his cap. Then he took the money and the watch, and ran home as fast as he could.

Meanwhile the two rogues went to the best inn in the town. They ordered a big dinner. When they had finished, they whirled Pekka's old cap in front of the innkeeper's eyes and asked, "Is everything paid for?"

"Of course it isn't!" cried the innkeeper.

"What do you mean?" cried the rogues. They whirled the cap again, and shouted, "Is everything paid for?"

"Are you crazy?" cried the innkeeper. "Or do you think you can make a fool of me? I'll soon show you!"

He fell upon the two rogues and gave them a good beating.

When Pekka reached home, he rushed into the hut and laid the watch, the money, and his fine new cap on the table. "What do you think of that?" he asked his father.

302

"But you never got all that for our old cow?"
Pekka grinned. "No," he said. "You see, I
sold my cap as well!"

James Cloyd Bowman AND *Margery Bianco*

WORD LIST

1774 different words appear in the stories in this book. This includes all variants, compounds, contractions, and proper names. Poetry is not included; pages where poetry occurs are starred (*).

1504 of these words have either been used in preceding books, or are among the first 2000 in the Thorndike word list. The word list below includes all the new words in the stories in this book that have a Thorndike rating of 3a or over. It also includes some new words that have a Thorndike rating lower than 3a. These words are in italics. They appear in the word list because, in spite of their low rating, they have sometimes presented problems either of pronunciation or of confusion with an even more familiar word.

320 new words are listed below.

TINKER'S ADVENTURES

1

2

3 Tinker's
adventures
tiger

4 crept
alas
toll-gate

5 mewed

6 *shoulder*
sprang
catnip
bundle
licked
whiskers

7 shone
hooted
purred

8 politely
stranger

9 prowl
beyond
knot
though

10 *

THE LITTLE SCARECROW BOY

11 Scarecrow
fierce

12 *terrible*

13 decided
frighten

14

15

16 *stretched*
whoa
backwards
feathers

17

18 *

OLD SNAPPER

19 Snapper
swamp
straight

20 mossy
nap

21

22 *creatures*
jaws

23 crawfish

24 swam

25 *slipping*

26 *believe*
exciting
bug
quite

80	oats		
	half		
81	combed		
	neighed		
82	rag		
	braided		
83	gid-ap		
	swung		
84	*sugar*		
	lumps		
	forward		
85			
86			
87			
88			
89	chin		
90			
91	*spread*		
92	yelled		
93	snorted		
	hind		
94	puppy		
95	hitch		
	buggy		
96			
97	reins		
98			
99			
100	*		

MR. TIMOTHY'S BOAT YARD

101	Mr. Timothy
	Michael
	clam
	dock
	mended
102	*stirring*
	knees
103	ho
	whirling
104	
105	drawer
	drill
106	mast
	boom
107	
108	
109	lucky
110	*thread*
	finally
	clapped
	ouch
111	
112	*sewed*
	dolly
	cart
113	aboard
114	ahead
115	*
116	*

MOVING DAY

117	
118	twisted
	hurray
119	giggle
120	chug-chugging
121	tunnel
122	bookcases
	slippers
123	ourselves
124	
125	sofa
	fourteenth
	wrist
126	*probably*
127	piano
128	*furniture*
129	
130	
131	
132	stove

THE LITTLE OLD COUNTRY CAR

133	rattled
	gas
	anybody
	garage
134	busses
	van
135	*sighed*

ACKNOWLEDGMENTS

For permission to use copyrighted material, thanks are due the following publishers and authors:

D. Appleton-Century Company, for "The Monkey and the Crocodile" and "Granny's Blackie," from *Jataka Tales*, by Ellen C. Babbitt.

Coward-McCann, Inc., for "The Tame Giraffe," from *Not Really!* by Lesley Frost.

Doubleday, Doran & Company, Inc., for "County Fair Day," from *A Little Book of Days*, by Rachel Field; and "Mice," from *Fifty-one New Nursery Rhymes*, by Rose Fyleman.

E. P. Dutton & Co., Inc., for "The Fish with the Deep Sea Smile" and "Sneakers," from *The Fish with the Deep Sea Smile*, by Margaret Wise Brown.

Harcourt, Brace, and Company, Inc., for "Little Blacknose," from *Little Blacknose*, by Hildegarde Hoyt Swift; and "Kittens' Questionnaire," from *Magpie Lane*, by Nancy Byrd Turner.

Florence Page Jaques, the author, and *Child Life*, for the poem "There Was Once a Puffin."

Little, Brown & Company, for "Take Away One" ("The Monkeys and the Crocodile"), from *Tirra Lirra*, by Laura E. Richards.

The Macmillan Company, for "The Little Turtle," from *Collected Poems*, by Vachel Lindsay; "Molly Whuppie," from *English Fairy Tales*, retold by Flora Annie Steel; and "The Falling Star," from *Collected Poems*, by Sara Teasdale.

G. P. Putnam's Sons, for "The Good Flea and the Wicked King," by Victor Hugo, adapted from *An Outline of Humor* edited by Carolyn Wells.

Frederick A. Stokes Company, for "The Elephant and the Whale" and "The Tortoise and the Elephant," from *Valery Carrick's Picture Folk-Tales*, by Valery Carrick.

Story Parade, for "Ebenezer Never-Could-Sneezer," by Gilbert S. Pattillo; "Runaway Song," by Mark Sawyer; and "The Tame Swan Talks to the Wild Swan," by Kathryn Worth.

Albert Whitman & Co., for "Pekka and the Rogues," from *Tales from a Finnish Tupa*, by James Cloyd Bowman and Margery Bianco.

Thanks are also due those authors of prose selections who have permitted slight editing of their material for further ease in reading.